FOURTH-GRADE CELEBRITY

PATRICIA REILLY GIFF

～∽∾～

Illustrated by Leslie Morrill

A YEARLING BOOK

FOR
200TH STREET
AND THE PEOPLE
WHO STILL LIVE THERE
IN MY MIND,
ESPECIALLY
MY MOTHER AND FATHER
AND ANNIE

Published by
Dell Yearling
an imprint of
Random House Children's Books
a division of Random House, Inc.
1540 Broadway
New York, New York 10036

Visit us on the Web! www.randomhouse.com/kids

Educators and librarians, for a variety of teaching tools,
visit us at www.randomhouse.com/teachers

ISBN: 0-440-41702-3

Reprinted by arrangement with Delacorte Press

Printed in the United States of America

September 2000

10 9 8 7 6 5 4 3 2 1

OPM

1

"Darlene Verona is a stinky, rotten thing for not inviting me to her birthday party," Casey said. She puffed out her cheeks and blew through her braces. "But if I were Darlene, I wouldn't invite me either."

Walter didn't answer.

"Hey, are you still there?" She peered through the Cyclone fence into the Secret Passageway, a space that ran in between the yards on 200th Street and the Ogden Schoolyard. It was a narrow alley filled with weeds and rocks and candy wrappers that the kids were always poking through the fence.

It was getting so dark, Casey could just about see Walter's green sweater. He was down on his hands and knees, looking into a hole he had dug in the center of the Passageway.

"I can't find them," he said finally. He pushed his

glasses higher on his nose. "I think they've disappeared."

Casey snorted. "Dead fish can't walk away. Keep looking."

Walter grunted.

She sat down on the grass, holding the book they kept for their science experiments, and leaned against the fence. "I know why Darlene didn't invite me. I have no zip. No style. I'm a lump of vanilla pudding."

"Nothing wrong with vanilla pudding. It's my favorite kind."

"Nothing wrong!" she said, her voice rising. "Nobody notices me. The school year is two weeks old and Mrs. Petty still calls me Vanessa. It's always my sister Van. Van is prettier. Van is smarter. Actually, what Van is is a pain in the A."

Walter looked up. "What brought this on all of a sudden?"

"Listen, Walt, all my life Van's been the perfect Valentine. It never bothered me that much before, but I've been thinking about it lately." She made a face. "Mrs. Petty made me bring home yesterday's work to be signed because it was kind of a mess. My mother carried on for ten minutes. All I heard about was my sister Van. How good she is in school—how terrific." She ran her tongue across her braces. "How disgusting."

Walter stopped digging. "I found them. I can see the corner of the can sticking out." He dug up a bright red coffee can and pried off the lid. "We shouldn't have started this so late. It's hard to get a good look at them."

"Do you want me to get a flashlight?"

2

"No, I guess they're about the same as they were last week." He poked his hand into the can. "Skin is still on them. Mark down 'no change' in the book."

"Good idea," she said. "We'll start earlier next week. And remember, it's my turn to check them out."

Walter pushed the can back into the hole and began to drop dirt in on top of it.

"Walt?" Casey said. "How about nominating me for class president?"

"I would, Casey," he said, brushing the dirt off his hands, "but I've already promised George Pomeroy I'd vote for him."

"I'll worry about that when we get to the voting part. How about it? I'll give you all my last year's baseball cards."

"Worthless."

"How about this year's?"

Walter climbed the fence and landed on her side with a thud.

"Look," she said. She squinted up at him, trying to see better in the dark. "I'm going to make myself over. Become a celebrity or something. But I need a little cooperation. By the end of this year I want everyone in school to know my name. At least. Let them know that Van isn't the only Valentine in school."

He stood there considering. "Get Tracy Matson off my back."

"Who?"

"Some idiot girl." He stopped to trim his thumbnail with his teeth. "She lived in the town where we stayed for a week on vacation last summer. Every time she sends me a letter, my mother makes me write back."

"And you'll nominate me tomorrow?"

Casey ran her tongue over her braces. "How can I—"

"Simple. She's just looking for a pen pal. Write and tell her you're a friend of mine. Say I can't write anymore, that my hand dropped off or something."

"And you'll nominate me tomorrow?"

"It's a deal. Walk me back to my house and I'll give you her address."

Casey stood up and dusted off the seat of her pants. "Let's go, Walter. Things are looking up already. A new pen pal and a nomination for class president practically in my pocket."

2

Dear Tracy Matson,

My name is Casey Valentine. I used to be Walter Moles's best friend. I know you will be sorry to learn that Walter passed on last night. He died heroically after capturing two kidnappers who were after me. (I'm rich.) I am having a gold medal made for his parents out of my allowance. ($500 per week.)

It's a shame that this happened now. We were conducting important experiments for the government (to see what happens to fish after they've been buried for a while).

Please do not write to Walter anymore. And don't write to his family. They want to forget about the whole thing. Write to me instead.

Your new friend,
Cassandra Eleanor Valentine

P.S. Before he died, Walter nominated me for class president.

3

Casey crammed the last of the apple pie into her mouth, washed most of it down with a gulp of milk, and rubbed the napkin across her face.

"May I be excused?" she asked her mother and scraped back the kitchen chair.

"Tell Van it's her night to do the dishes."

"With pleasure."

"And, Casey . . ."

She waited on one foot.

"Push the hair out of your eyes."

She gave her bangs a quick swipe with her hand and took the stairs to the bedroom two at a time. "Are you in there, Van?"

Her older sister was standing on tiptoe on the footboard of her bed, balancing herself with her fingertips on the ceiling.

"Mother said—" Casey began.

"Shut up a minute, will you, Casey? How am I ever going to get to be an Olympic gymnast with all these interruptions?"

Casey watched Van inch her way across the footboard. Her sister was a great athlete, even though there were fingerprints all over the ceiling. She was the smartest kid in sixth grade, too. There was no doubt about it. Van was a genius.

"It's your night to do the dishes," Casey said as Van reached the end of the footboard.

"It's always my night to do the dishes." Van did a flip off the edge of the footboard, landed upright, then stood on her head.

"Why do you have to do that all the time?" Casey asked.

"Keeping fit," Van answered, smoothing her short blond hair.

Casey flopped across her own bed. "I'll do you a little favor and do the dishes tonight if you want."

"What do I have to do?"

"Write a limerick for me."

"Are you kidding? I thought you were going to be a writer when you grow up."

"A sensible writer—mystery stories, stuff like that," Casey said. "But I have to have a limerick for Monday. All I can think of is 'There was an old man from—' "

"That's a good start."

"Come on, Vanny."

"Sorry, Casey, I just finished my own homework and I'm not much good at those things. You're the one with imagination."

Van stood on her head.

"Please?"

Van cocked her head to one side. "You look like a schnauzer with your hair hanging over your eyes like that."

Casey blew her hair off her forehead. "Can't help it. I'm trying to get it to grow long like Darlene's." She glanced in the mirror and dragged her bangs back as hard as she could. "See, they just won't stay." She turned around so Van could watch her brown hair pop back over her forehead.

"I don't know why you want to get rid of your bangs, anyway."

"Nobody in my class wears bangs anymore."

"I don't want to hurt your feelings, but I think you look better with bangs. Hides some of your freckles. Makes your face a little prettier."

Casey looked back at the mirror. Her face was long, and skinny like the rest of her. Not nearly as pretty as Darlene's. She turned and stuck her tongue out at Van, feeling hurt. "You don't look so hot either, Van. You're starting to get pimples. You'll probably have a face like a pan of worms by next year."

Van made a face and picked a banana peel off the radio. "I'm not going to clean this mess of a room again." She tossed the peel into the wastebasket. "What a slob you are, Casey. I wish I could move up to the attic and room by myself."

"I wish you could too," Casey said to her sister's back as Van went downstairs to do the dishes.

Casey wandered over to her closet, grabbed a pile of clothes, and draped them on her bed.

Look, she said to herself, you'd better wear something a little special tomorrow. She held a pair of tan pants in front of her and glanced in the mirror. "Look like a camel," she muttered and dropped them on the floor. She picked up her blue-plaid pants and scratched at a powdery white stain that covered one knee. Most of it came off, but there was still a grayish spot underneath.

She spit on it and rubbed a little harder. She'd have to wait and see it when it dried. She hung it over her pink lamp shade and tried to decide on something else, just in case.

The trouble was that everything was a little spotty or a little ripped. She couldn't understand it. Two weeks ago, before school started, her mother had taken her to Susan's Discount Shop for a bunch of new stuff. Now everything was a mess. And these clothes weren't nearly as great as the cashier lady had said they were. No one in the class seemed to be wearing pastel shirts and plaid pants.

She left the clothes in a pile on the bed. Carry a pocketbook, she advised herself, and hold it right over the stain on the blue slacks. No one will ever notice.

She looked doubtfully at the stain, then walked over to Van's closet. Locked again. She wiggled the knob.

She tiptoed to the top of the stairs and leaned over. Van was doing the dishes. She could hear her talking with Mom.

Grinning, she sped back into the bedroom and began to search. She looked under Van's mattress, in her jewelry box, and under the lamp on her night table.

Finally she stood in the center of the room and twirled around slowly. "Where is that key?" she whispered. She turned around again and pounced on the wastebasket in the corner. Bending over, she lifted it until she saw the silver gleam of the key.

"Aha, foolish Van," she said, twisting an imaginary mustache. "Nevair can you fool zee great Inspector Valentine." Smiling, she rolled her tongue over her braces. If that stain didn't fade out a little, she'd borrow something of Van's.

One problem solved. Then she frowned. There was still the limerick gnawing at her. "There was an old man named—" She sat cross-legged in the middle of Van's bed. "There was a young man—"

It was a shame she had to waste her time on such a ratty assignment. There was an important list she wanted to make and a book she wanted to finish. The book was a great mystery, and she was sure she knew who had hidden the letter in the old trunk. She just had to find out if she was right. She picked up the book and began to read.

An hour later Van was back. "Do you have to peel your nail polish off all over the bed?" she said. "And why do you have to lie on my bed all the time, anyway?"

Casey looked up guiltily. "Too much junk on mine. Besides, I meant to lie here and read for only a few minutes. What time is it?"

"Nine thirty."

Casey slammed the book shut and stood up. "Darn. I have to wash my hair."

"Mother said to get ready for bed."

"I'll hurry. I have to look good tomorrow. Mrs. Petty

is going to announce the results of the election for class president. And I'm one of the candidates."

"You?"

"Yes, me."

"Hey, that's pretty good. I hope you win. Who nominated you?"

Casey scraped some more Blue Torch nail polish off her thumb. "Walter."

"How did you get him to do that?"

"None of your business."

Van shrugged and picked up the blue-plaid pants. "What's this filthy thing doing on the lamp?"

"Is it? Filthy, I mean?"

"Look at this big stain."

"Vanny, how about doing me a little favor?"

Van glanced at her closet door. "Don't you dare touch any of my clothes."

"The closet's locked. How can I?" she asked, carefully keeping her eyes away from the wastebasket.

"And it's going to stay locked too," Van said emphatically, "or my closet will be a wreck just like yours. Do you know I saw an old dried-up liverwurst sandwich on your closet floor before?"

Casey grabbed her pajamas from under her pillow and went down the hall to the bathroom, muttering, "There was a young lady from—"

It wasn't until she was back in bed, thinking about the liverwurst sandwich and trying to remember when she'd left it there, that she realized Van had been in her closet.

"Hey. Why were you—" she began, leaning up on one elbow, but Van was sound asleep.

4

WAYS TO BECOME A CELEBRITY

BY

CASSANDRA ELEANOR VALENTINE

1. Become class president.
2. Rescue child, cat, dog, etc., from burning building.
3. Do something different, unusual, like speaking French.
4. Become an athlete. Do 100 pull-ups on W.M.'s bar in garage.
5. Get name in paper.

14

Ways to become a celebrity.

5

The next morning Casey chewed each mouthful of cereal ten times and spread three coats of Blue Torch polish on her nails. Finally Van left for school without her.

Fifteen minutes later Casey skipped out of the house dressed in Van's green corduroy jumper and ice-blue shirt. Cutting across Walter's lawn next door to get to the Ogden School gate, she reflected that it was pretty convenient living only two houses away from the entrance to the school. The bell had rung, but she caught the line into her class before it reached the second floor.

She cut in ahead of Gunther Reed.

"Think you're going to win today?" he asked.

Ordinarily she didn't speak to him, but today she smiled. "I hope so."

"Acting pretty friendly all of a sudden," he said. "Think I'm going to vote for you?"

"Don't bother," she said and turned her back on him.

She sat down at her table and arranged Van's jumper carefully underneath her so it wouldn't wrinkle. Then she rooted around in her drawer for a pencil and a piece of paper.

She smoothed the edge of the paper and wrote in her best handwriting:

A LIMERICK

BY

CASSANDRA ELEANOR VALENTINE

She saw a shadow on her paper and looked up. Mrs. Petty stood there watching her. Her round face was reddish and her front teeth, slightly separated, rested on her lower lip.

"That's homework, Van—er—Cassandra," she said, spraying slightly as she said the *s*'s.

Casey nodded and put the limerick paper away. She looked at the blackboard. Four jobs to do this morning, she calculated. Arithmetic, social studies, science, and art.

She took out her math book. Leafing through, she found page 27. She sighed. It was the worst: long division. Not because she didn't know how to do it. She did. In fact, sometimes it was interesting to estimate all over the place and finally come up with something close. The trouble was that there were so many chances to make mistakes because of all that multiplying and subtracting.

She ripped a page out of her loose-leaf notebook and began to divide. She worked as fast as she could because she was in a hurry to get to the social studies assignment. She was supposed to pretend she had traveled across the prairie in a covered wagon and was writing to a friend back East to tell about her adventures. It was the kind of assignment she loved. She intended to put in lots of danger, with hostile Indians kidnapping her and wild beasts chasing her every step of the way to California.

She worked her way through the morning, stopping occasionally to think about the class election. If she won, she'd consider it a sign that her whole life would change. Everybody would stop thinking Van was so perfect and start to realize that she, Casey, was pretty important too.

Finally she took out the page she had labeled for her limerick, thought for a moment, then scribbled something down that almost rhymed:

> There once were two Valentine girls.
> The oldest one seemed like a pearl.
> She could stand on her head
> At the foot of the bed,
> But she wasn't so hot after all.

Then she sat back and sucked air through her braces to make a swishing noise while she waited for Mrs. Petty to announce the winner of the fourth-grade election for class president.

It seemed to take forever. Not that she thought she had much chance of winning. In fact, she probably had no chance at all. She knew of only two people in the class who had voted for her—Mindy Gregory, who was another blob of vanilla pudding, and Casey herself. And she really wasn't so sure about Mindy's vote. Lately Mindy had done a lot of smiling at George Pomeroy, and since he was running, too . . .

Suddenly she stopped swishing. Suppose Mindy hadn't voted for her? And suppose no one else had voted for her? Even though she had disguised her handwriting carefully, making big wavery letters uphill across the page, it would be pretty obvious to the whole class that she had voted for herself.

Mrs. Petty rapped a plump hand on the edge of the desk. She stood there fiddling with the large white beads she always wore.

"Boys and girls," she said finally, "if everyone is finished with his boardwork, we'll discuss the class election now. I've just finished counting the votes."

Casey swished gently and looked out the window as if she weren't particularly interested in the results.

"We have a problem with this election," Mrs. Petty said. "The winner was Catherine Wilson. But Catherine will be out of school for the next few weeks with a broken leg, so we really can't wait for her to come back. We need a president now."

Casey looked back at her with interest. Maybe she had a chance.

Mrs. Petty twisted her beads. "The runner-up was George Pomeroy."

Casey shot an accusing look at Mindy's back, two seats in front of her.

"But," Mrs. Petty said, "Mrs. Pomeroy called this

morning. Unfortunately, the Pomeroys are moving very shortly. . . ." She broke off and smiled at George. "We'll really miss you. However," she continued, "we still need a class president. The only candidate left is Cassandra Valentine."

Casey swished once in pure joy.

"No fair," Gunther yelled from the back of the room.

Mrs. Petty looked at him. "That will do, Gunther."

"She probably had only one vote." He snickered. "Her own."

Darlene Verona raised her hand. "How many votes did Casey have, anyway?" she asked.

Mrs. Petty hesitated.

Casey sank down in her seat. Gunther was probably right, she thought bitterly.

"Maybe we should start over, pull a name out of a hat or something," Darlene went on. "I'm not sure Casey is really the people's choice, anyway."

"Right," someone in the back of the room said.

Mrs. Petty clapped her hands. "Well—maybe that's what we should do. Yes. We'll put everyone's name in a box and choose the class president that way. We'll have to hurry, though—it's almost lunchtime."

Casey was so disappointed she could hardly tear a little piece of paper out of her assignment pad to write her name for the box. Slowly she sharpened her pencil in her rocket sharpener.

With her pencil, not even bothering to disguise her handwriting, she wrote in big letters: CASSANDRA VALENTINE. She folded the paper carefully in half and dropped it into the box Mrs. Petty was passing around the room.

She folded the paper and dropped it into the box.

6

Twenty minutes later, in the cafeteria, Casey slid her tray along the rack with one hand and fished for her lunch ticket with the other.

"Just a minute," she told Betty, the cook. "It's in my wallet somewhere."

Betty wiped her hand across her forehead. "Fourth time you've lost your ticket in two weeks."

Behind Casey a six-grader groaned. "Hurry up, will you? By the time I get off this line, lunch will be over."

"Wait a minute," Casey said over her shoulder. "Doing the best I can."

She dug deeper into the zippered compartment of her wallet and held up a wrinkled blue lunch ticket. "Told you it was here." She dropped it on the counter and slid some change on top of it.

"Think I'll treat myself to an extra hot dog." She smiled at the cook. "It's a special day."

"Birthday?"

Casey shook her head. "No. I was elected class president this morning."

Someone in the back of the line groaned again. "Come on. Move."

Betty plunked the hot dogs on the tray. Casey picked it up and went to one of the fourth-grade tables. For a moment she stood there uncertainly. Today she had been last in her class line. She hated it when that happened. It meant that all the kids were seated ahead of her, hunched over their sandwiches, talking to each other. No one would pay attention to her standing there or move over for her to sit down.

"Any room here?" she asked, squeezing on the end next to Mindy Gregory. She nodded to Walter, who was at the other end of the table, leaning against the wall.

"Bought myself two hot dogs today in honor of the occasion," she told Mindy.

"What occasion?" Mindy asked through her milk straw.

"Being elected class president. Did you forget already?"

Gunther Reed, on the other side of the table, looked at Casey and hooted. "I wouldn't call having your name picked out of a box being elected."

"Shut up, Goony," Casey answered. She took a huge bite of her hot dog. This had been some morning. By the time Mrs. Petty had chosen George Pomeroy to pull a name out of the box, Casey had almost given up. She held her breath while George gave the paper he had picked to the teacher.

Mrs. Petty unfolded the paper so slowly it seemed to take an hour.

Finally she looked directly at Casey. "Well, well," she said. "It's Van—I mean, Cassandra Valentine."

"Me!" Casey said.

"What do you mean—me?" Mindy asked in a loud voice.

Casey jumped. She had almost forgotten she was in the cafeteria, eating her lunch.

"Sorry, Mindy. I guess I was daydreaming. Thinking of being elected—I mean, picked out of the box."

Gunther made a rude noise. "I suppose this is all we're going to hear about through the whole lunch hour."

"Shut up, Goony," Casey and Mindy said together.

Encouraged because this was the first time anyone had stuck up for her against Gunther, Casey grinned at Mindy. "Maybe you can help me this year," she said. "You could be sort of a deputy or something."

"Luuuck-y," Gunther said, drawing the word out.

"Why do you have to sit here all the time, Goony, when you're such a pest?" Casey asked.

"I was here first," he said. "Remember? Half of your behind is still in the aisle."

"What took you so long to get down to lunch today, anyway?" Mindy asked.

"Mrs. Petty wanted to see me."

"About what?"

"About being class president. She said I'd have to be a model now."

Gunther made a face. "Some model you are, Tinsel Teeth."

Casey blushed. "I can't help wearing braces. Besides, Mrs. Petty meant a model of good behavior, not a model like in the magazines."

"Good thing." He snorted and swung his legs over the bench, overhanded the remains of his lunch into the wastebasket, and disappeared out the door leading to the schoolyard.

"Don't pay any attention to him, Casey," Mindy said. She looked at Casey critically. "When those braces come off, your teeth will probably look as good as everybody else's."

Casey winced and ran her tongue across the top of her hot dog. "Why does school mustard always taste so yucky?"

Mindy shrugged. She seemed more interested in listening to Darlene Verona on her other side tell about how great her birthday party was going to be.

Casey pretended she couldn't hear. Anyway, she was relieved that Mindy hadn't asked what else Mrs. Petty had said. She really didn't want anyone to know, except maybe Walter, who always listened and never had much to say.

Just before lunch Mrs. Petty had crooked her finger at Casey, and as the rest of the class started to file out of the room to the cafeteria, she motioned for Casey to sit on the chair next to her desk.

"Well, Van," she said, smiling, "you got to be president, after all."

"Casey."

"Yes indeed, Cassandra. You'll have some big responsibilities this year. I hope you're up to them."

Casey lowered her head. Mrs. Petty was spraying the desk lightly with *s*'s as she talked.

"I think you'll make a good leader," Mrs. Petty continued, "that is, if you can pull yourself together. Some of your ideas are a little . . ." She paused and looked up at the ceiling. "A little peculiar."

If only Mrs. Petty could learn to speak without using the letter *s* so often, Casey thought. Or maybe she could work it out so she wouldn't have to say it at all. She could call children with *s* in their names "dear," and say things like "want" instead of "wish." Too bad the principal's name was Mr. Rosenstrauss. She really couldn't call him "dear. . . ."

"Cassandra," Mrs. Petty said sharply.

Casey jumped. "Yes, Mrs. Petty."

"Do you understand?"

Casey tried to remember what Mrs. Petty had just said. By the look of the desk, whatever it was must have had plenty of *s*'s in it. Finally she gave up. "Be neater?"

"What I'm saying, Cassandra, is that you have to be a model for the rest of the twenty-two people in this room. Be more—well, more like your sister Van."

Casey gritted her teeth.

Mrs. Petty fiddled with her beads. "Well, you'll be late for lunch. Do the best you can this year."

Casey stood up.

"And do try to be a little neater, dear. A good president is careful, remember?"

Casey had nodded one last time and sped out the door toward the lunchroom.

"Hey, Casey," Mindy said, "you've been dreaming this whole lunch hour. Pay attention."

Casey picked up her other hot dog and started to eat. She ducked as she saw her sister Van go by with her best friend, Sue Verona, Darlene's older sister.

Then her eyes widened. Van, that weasel, was carrying Casey's canvas pocketbook. So that's what Van had been doing in her closet when she found the liverwurst sandwich.

Casey stood up. But then she remembered she was wearing Van's jumper. She wiped a little mustard off the front of it and sat down again.

Darlene leaned across Mindy. "Your sister Van got to be president of her class, too."

"How do you know?"

"Met my sister Susan in the girls' room. She said that practically everyone in the class voted for Van."

Casey pushed the last of her hot dog into her mouth and stood up, chewing. "I guess we can go outside until the bell rings," she said as soon as she could talk.

7

Friday after school Casey took the back steps two at a time, nudged the door open, and dropped her books in the kitchen. She reached for the largest apple in the bowl on the table, but switched to a smaller one when she noticed a brown spot on the bottom. Probably full of worms, she thought. Leave it for Van.

She sniffed. What was that smell? She walked into the hall and peered into the living room. Cans of paint and drop cloths all over the place. It looked as if the whole house would be in a mess for days.

Her mother sat on the couch staring at little cards of different colors.

Casey leaned over her. "What are they?"

"Paint samples," her mother answered. "We're going

"What are they?" Casey asked.

to do the living room in beige." She held a gray card up in the air and squinted at it. "Can't decide on a color for the hall, though."

"Pretty dull, if you ask me," Casey said.

Her father appeared in the doorway. "What do you want, Casey? Polka dots?"

Casey looked up at him and giggled. "Aren't you home from work early?"

"I had some extra time off coming," he answered, "so I thought I'd get a start on the painting. You and Van better get together and decide on a color for your room."

Casey stood there considering. "Why does it have to be one color?" she said thoughtfully. "Maybe we should do it in wide stripes. We could use the Olympic colors—you know, a stripe of blue, yellow, black, then a stripe of green, red."

"Leave it to you, Casey," said Van from the hall. "Who ever heard of all those colors in one room? I vote for a pale blue."

"No one around here has any imagination at all," Casey grumbled.

"I might have a tough time painting all those stripes anyway, Casey," her father said, grinning. "You have a couple of days to decide, girls. I'm going to do the living room first."

Casey shrugged. "I'm going out then. We'll talk about it later." She stood up and wandered out to the kitchen. On the counter was a pink envelope. It was a letter from Tracy Matson. Casey folded it in half and tucked it in her pocket.

A minute later she climbed the fence to the Secret Passageway, pausing to yell for Walter over her shoulder. Then she settled herself on a pile of leaves and leaned back against the fence.

She looked up to see Walter loping down the driveway.

"Hi, Prez," he said as he vaulted the fence. "So you got to be a celebrity, after all."

"Between you and me, things were pretty close there for a while." She looked through the fence into the schoolyard, where Gunther was riding his bicycle, and frowned. "Mostly because of that rat, Goony Reed. But I shouldn't complain—I probably got only one vote anyway. Then I got in by the skin of my teeth, picked out of a box, as Goony said. But good old Van had about a thousand people voting for her." She sucked on her braces in annoyance.

"I voted for you."

"Are you kidding, Walt?" she asked, immediately cheering up. She took a bite out of her apple and held the other side up to him.

He shook his head.

"Go on, it's good." She wiped her mouth with the back of her hand. "So I got to be president, but there's a lot more to being a celebrity than this. I told you, I want everybody in the school to know my name, instead of saying, 'That's Van Valentine's little sister,' all the time. But it's going to take some figuring to see how I'm going to manage . . ." She broke off. "Are you listening to me?"

"Trying to see if I can set these leaves on fire." He held up a magnifying glass. "Get the sun to shine through in the right way and—"

"And the next thing you know," she cut in, "you'll burn down the whole neighborhood. Hey, I almost forgot, more good news."

He looked up.

"I have here," she said, reaching into her pocket, "my very first letter from my very first pen pal."

"Big deal, Lucille."

"Very funny. Let me see what she has to say." She tore open the envelope and lowered her head over the letter. Then she looked up. "Good grief. Wait till you see the mess we're in now. It's a good thing my mother doesn't read my mail. She'd kill me."

He leaned over and took the letter out of her hands.

Dear Cassandra Eleanor:

Thank you for writting to me. I hope you write more often then Walter did.

I'm sorry to hear about Walter. Did they shoot him, or what? My mother is going to write a letter to Mrs. Moles to tell her she feels terruble or she may even send flowers.

I am in the 4th grade in the Thaddeus Lowell School. I'm a grate swimmer and I'm the best fisherman in the town of High Flats.

How are you? I hope you are fine. I am so glad that you are writting to me. I never had a rich fiend before. I've told everyone in my class about you and they are waiting to read your letters.

I guess a rich kid like you has a lot of things to do. I have a lot of things to do too.

Write soon.

Your fiend,
Tracy

P.S. I hope you were elected class president.

Walter trimmed the edge of his thumbnail with his teeth. "Kid can't spell too well."

"What are we going to do?" Casey asked.

"I think we should have told her my hand dropped off."

"Ha, ha," Casey answered. She picked up a pebble and threw it through a hole in the Cyclone fence. "Maybe we could send another letter. Tell her the whole town has the plague. People are dying off like flies, and your parents were buried last—"

"Listen, Casey, the florist's truck could pull up at my door any minute. Remember, Tracy must have written this letter a couple of days ago." He checked the postmark on the envelope. "I told you that girl is nothing but a pest."

For a moment there was silence. Casey picked up a stick and started a ticktacktoe in the dirt. "Maybe we'd better go sit on your front steps," she said finally.

He stood up. "Right. We'll wait for the florist and wave him off or something."

Together they hopped the fence and started down the driveway.

Mrs. Moles was standing at her back door. "Where have you been?" she asked Walter. "I've been calling for the last ten minutes. It's time to eat." She turned to Casey. "Pancakes and sausages for supper. Want to stay?"

Casey hesitated, weighing the pancakes, which she loved, against going home and trying to forget about the florist and what would happen when he arrived at the Moleses' house.

"Er . . ." she said at last, deciding in favor of the pancakes, "I'll stay."

Mrs. Moles laughed. "It doesn't sound as if you're wildly enthusiastic."

Casey felt her cheeks redden. "I didn't mean—"

"Just teasing," Mrs. Moles said. "Run and tell your mother."

Five minutes later Casey stood in the Moles kitchen, scooping knives and forks out of the drawer while Walter fed his cat, Carrots.

"We'll set the dining-room table tonight," Mrs. Moles said.

Casey stopped scooping. "Someone's birthday?"

"No, Walter's grandmother is staying with us for a few days. And"—she stopped to check the sausages sizzling on the stove—"I received a beautiful little bouquet of flowers today. It looks too pretty for the kitchen. Go take a look."

Casey laid the silverware gently on the counter and went into the dining room. In the middle of the table was a small bowl of yellow daisies.

Mrs. Moles's voice trailed after her. ". . . a lovely thing to do. But I can't understand—hardly know the people."

Casey leaned back against the wall and gulped. "Beautiful," she said, "just beautiful."

At dinner Walter sat across the table from her. Every time Casey looked at him she wondered if he felt as guilty as she did. Walter's grandmother, Mrs. Thorrien, kept saying how lovely the daisies were, and Mrs. Moles kept wondering why Mrs. Matson would want to send them flowers.

"There was no message on the card," Mrs. Moles said, shaking her head. "It was simply signed Janet and Robert Matson."

"Bunch of nuts, if you ask me," Walter said.

Casey felt a giggle coming and quickly turned to Mrs. Thorrien. "Do you think you could teach me some words?"

Mrs. Thorrien looked at her over her glasses. "I am," she said, "hard of hearing. Did you say words?"

"Yes."

"Words." Mrs. Thorrien nodded. "What kind?"

"Any kind."

"Mother," Mrs. Moles yelled, "I think Casey means in French."

"Oh." Mrs. Thorrien nodded again. "I understand now. *Mais oui.* Yes."

Casey waited expectantly.

Mrs. Thorrien said something very rapidly in French.

"What does that mean?"

"I like these pretty flowers."

Casey rolled her eyes at Walter and finished the rest of her pancakes.

35

8

It was a good thing Walter had an appointment with the dentist. From her bedroom window Casey had seen him drive away with his mother. She had thrown on some clothes and raced through breakfast, thinking this was the perfect time to try out his chinning bar. No sense letting him know she was determined to do more pull-ups than Jim Williams, the best athlete in the school—at least not until she had practiced a little.

She trotted down Walter's driveway and pulled open the heavy garage doors. Walter's mother and father certainly were the tidiest people in the neighborhood. Their tools and paint cans were stacked neatly on the shelves, and the rake and broom hung on hooks. Near the front of the garage, nailed to two beams, was the chinning bar.

She stood in front of it, eyes narrowed. Someday

Van would be standing on her head thinking she was some kind of athletic genius. And someone would come along and say, "Hey, have you heard about Casey? Forty-four pull-ups today and not even out of breath. I guess it must be hard to have a sister who's so terrific."

Slowly she spit on her hands and wiped them on her jeans. Stretching her arms over her head, she leaped for the bar. For a minute she hung there, swinging gently, before she tried to raise her head over the top.

Not too easy, she thought. She could only get the top of her head as high as the bar. No, not easy at all. She loosened her grip on the bar and collapsed on the garage floor.

"Never get to be a celebrity athlete this way," she said as she pushed herself to her feet.

"You can say that again," a voice said behind her.

She jumped and spun around. "Gunther Reed. Why are you spying on me?"

"Spying?" He grinned. "Ball went over the school-yard fence." He held it up. "Landed in the Moleses' backyard." He started down the driveway, then called back over his shoulder, "You, a celebrity?" Cackling horribly, he loped down the street toward his house.

"You big pineapple!" she yelled after him.

She turned and looked at the bar. "Lousy idea any-way. Have to think of something else. Too bad I can't knock out Gunther Reed's front teeth. Then I'd really be a celebrity. Probably even his mother wouldn't mind."

She stood for a minute trying to decide what she could do while she waited for Walter. Maybe she should dig up the fish, just check them out and see

37

She hung there, swinging gently.

what was doing with them. She took a step toward the Secret Passageway and hesitated. It really wouldn't be fair. She'd kill Walter if he dug them up without her.

Behind her she heard a car door slam. Quickly she dusted off her hands. "Back already?" she asked Walter as he trudged down the driveway toward her.

"Already?" He scowled. "You wouldn't have thought it was so fast if you'd been tortured by the dentist for an hour." He put his finger in his mouth and rubbed his gum gently.

She touched her own braces sympathetically. "You think I don't know? Best thing is not to think about it. Come on, let's look at the fish."

"Again? We dug them up the other day."

"So what? There's nothing else to do. Boringest Saturday morning I've had in ten years."

He hesitated. "I really should get my papers delivered early today. I want to stop and ask a lot of weekday people to take the Sunday paper."

"Why do you have to waste your time on that now? I've been hanging around this yard all morning. Not a thing to do, just waiting for you to get home."

"The kid who adds the most new customers to the Sunday paper gets a prize."

"Money?"

"No. You get to have lunch with the famous reporter Lance Levan."

"Really?"

"Yeah," Walter said. "The kid who won last year said it was the best lunch he ever had. He ate four desserts and started on a fifth. When he couldn't finish it, they packed it up in a box for him to take home."

"I guess everybody in the country knows Lance Levan's name," Casey said dreamily. "It must be something to be a famous reporter. Hey, I wonder—"

"What?"

"Let me think about it awhile. I have to ask Mrs. Petty if it's all right. It might be just what I'm looking for in this celebrity business. But listen, Walt, I've got to do something with myself this morning, and if you're so determined to sell newspapers, I'm going to dig up those fish by myself."

He stood there, undecided. Then he nodded. "Who am I kidding, anyway? After I go through a big speech with the first three customers, I'd be sick of the whole thing and give it up anyway. Wait till I get the shovel." He took down the spade that was hanging neatly against the garage wall. "Let's go."

They hurdled the fence and started to dig. Five minutes later they still hadn't found the bright red coffee can. "Strange," Walter said.

"Keep digging," Casey said. "Bound to be here. Same thing happened last time. There, I see the edge of it now."

"Yeah. But look where it is. We didn't put it all the way over here next to the fence."

"Don't be silly. We must have." She knelt down and pried out the can. "Sit down a minute and rest while I take a look."

He wiped his forehead and squatted next to the fence as she ran her fingers under the lid of the can.

"I hate to tell you," she said as she looked in the can, "but they don't seem to be in here."

He leaned over to look. "You're right. Holy moly. What's that?"

"A piece of slimy paper." She reached in under the lid, pulled it out, and read:

IF YOU WANT THEM BACK,

LEAVE 50¢ IN THE CAN.

SIGNED,

THE FISHNAPPER

HA. HA.

"Hey," she said, outraged. "What nerve!"

"Who—"

"Who do you think? I'll bet anything it was Goony Reed."

"Do you think so?"

"Of course. He's going to turn out to be a real criminal someday, if you ask me. We'll pick up the newspaper and there he'll be, smack on the front page." She tossed the can back into the hole. "Throw some dirt on it, Walt. Let him dig it up again before he finds out we didn't put the money in it."

Walter tossed a shovelful of dirt on the can. Leaning on the handle of the spade, he said, "He's really not so bad. Just wants to make you pay attention to him."

"He certainly doesn't know how to go about it."

Walter threw another pile of dirt over the hole and stamped on it.

Casey got up to help him flatten the dirt. "The whole world will know Gunther's name someday," she said. "I can see the headlines—'Gunther Reed Sentenced to

41

Life Imprisonment for Ripping off the First National Bank.' Yes, and I probably won't ever be a celebrity even in my own school."

"That reminds me." Walter reached into his pocket and brought out a crumpled piece of paper. "I've got something for you."

"I hope it's not another pen pal. I'm having enough trouble keeping up with Tracy Matson."

Walter shook his head. "No pen pal. It's from my grandmother. I forgot to give it to you."

She unfolded the paper and smoothed it out.

Dear Casey,

Here are some words for you. When you know them, I will be happy to give you some more.

Sincerely,
Marie Thorrien

The French word is:	You say it this way:	It means:
un . . . deux . . . trois	uhn . . . duh . . . trwah	1 . . . 2 . . . 3
Bonjour	bohn zhoor	hello
Au revoir	oh ra-vwahr	good-bye
Je m'appelle Casey.	Zhuh ma-pehl Casey.	My name is Casey.

Casey sat there, running her tongue along her braces. Then, flicking the paper with her index finger, she looked up at Walter. "Do you know anybody in the class who speaks French?"

He shook his head and threw a pebble through a hole in the fence.

"Darlene Pain-in-the-A Verona?"

"No."

"And how about my sister Van?"

"You know she doesn't—" he began and picked up another pebble.

"No," she said, answering her own question. "Nobody does except"—she paused and put her hands on her hips—"Zee Great Ca-sey, Fourth Grade Cee-le-bri-ty."

He tossed another pebble at a tree on the other side of the fence and grunted.

She stood up and dusted off her pants. "See you later. I'm going in the house to memorize these words. Get hold of your grandmother as soon as you can. Tell her to write out a new list. Tell her she can put twice as many words on the next list. Get it for tomorrow. And, Walt—"

"Yeah?"

"Tell her to write some sentences. Some nice long important sentences."

She stuck one foot into a hole in the Cyclone fence and swung the other leg over the top. "Oh ra-vwahr, old boy, I'll see you later."

9

As the class filed out of the room at lunchtime on Monday, Casey paused at the classroom door. She took one last look at the list Walter had given her this morning from his grandmother. She had almost memorized the twelve new French words on it. Mrs. Petty was still sitting at her desk marking the English compositions they had done that morning. Casey wondered if she ever ate lunch. She certainly was fat enough to skip it.

"What is it, Cassandra?" Mrs. Petty asked, looking up.

Casey cleared her throat. "I was thinking about getting a newspaper together—sell it to the kids in school —get some money for the class treasury for trips and stuff."

"That's a very good idea," Mrs. Petty said in a slightly surprised voice.

"But we'd need some help," Casey went on. "Paper and permission to use the ditto machine in the office."

Mrs. Petty reached into her desk drawer and pulled out a bulging paper bag. "That shouldn't be much of a problem." She put a fat ham hero and two packages of chocolate crackers on the desk. Casey's mouth watered.

"I guess you'd like me to be the editor," Mrs. Petty suggested.

"Er, not exactly. I thought, being the class president and all, that I'd—"

Mrs. Petty took a bite of the sandwich and started to chew. "This English composition you wrote this morning doesn't seem to be the work of a newspaper editor."

"I couldn't think of anything I did over the weekend that was interesting enough to write about."

Mrs. Petty sat there rolling the hunk of sandwich from one side of her mouth to the other. She swallowed. "All right," she said at last. "Get a committee together and let's see how it goes."

"I will," Casey answered, relieved. "Right away."

"Make sure you get some people who can write well. Like Darlene, perhaps."

Casey nodded.

"And ask Gunther."

"Gunther Reed?"

"Be sure to put him in on this. Be good for him."

She leaned over and took another bite of sandwich. "This newspaper business may teach you a little effi-

Casey's mouth watered.

ciency also, Cassandra. Now go down and get some lunch before the hour is up."

Casey sped down to the cafeteria, her sneakers pounding on the stairs. That Gunther Reed. That turkey.

She grabbed up a tray and slipped into the lunch line, making a face at the gooey chow mein Betty dumped on her plate.

When she got to the fourth-grade table, she pushed hard against Mindy to make room and slid onto the edge of the bench. "Listen, kids," she said. "We're going to have a class newspaper."

No one heard her. All the kids were hunched over their plates, trying to slide the chow mein onto their forks.

"Hey, listen." She took her fork and banged on the side of her tray.

Darlene looked up and nudged the girls on each side of her with her elbows.

"We're going to have a class newspaper," Casey repeated when most of the kids stopped talking. "Mrs. Petty said we could. Everybody can write for it, but we need a committee who'll do most of the work." She paused to take a sip of milk. "I'm supposed to pick the committee."

Suddenly everyone was quiet. She looked down the table questioningly at Walter, but he shook his head. No surprise. Walter hated anything to do with writing.

Darlene leaned across the table. "Pick me," she whispered. "Come on."

Casey narrowed her eyes and looked at her.

"That reminds me," Darlene continued. "I forgot to

47

ask you to my birthday party. Completely slipped my mind."

Casey hesitated. Then when Darlene had almost given up, she said, "*Naturellement*, my dear Darlene, I was going to ask you anyway. And . . . I'll come to your party, too." She tried not to giggle.

She looked around the table again. It was clear that Mindy was dying to be picked. Good idea actually. Mindy would be the only one who wouldn't fight to be boss. "Mindy," she said, and was pleased to see Mindy's face light up. "One more, I guess," she said, delaying, hating to add Gunther to the group.

At last she looked at him. "How about you, Goony?"

He pretended to fall backward off the bench.

"Well," she said grudgingly, "Mrs. Petty suggested—"

For a moment he didn't answer. Then: "I might have known. Mrs. Petty said I had to be on the committee. Right?"

She ignored him. "We have to get together to have a meeting. How about my house on Friday?"

"Why wait so long?" Darlene asked.

"House is being painted. I'm not allowed to have kids in while my father is painting. Ladders and stuff all over the place."

"We don't have to have it at your house," Gunther said.

"He's right," Darlene agreed. "Let's not wait so long."

"Uh-uh," Casey said. If they went to his house, he'd be able to hog the whole thing. "I'm the editor. We'll have it at my house. Keep the records and stuff there."

Gunther laughed rudely. "Watch out or you'll be the editor of a newspaper that nobody will pay any attention to. I'll start a rival one."

Mindy looked nervous. "Let's not ruin this before it even gets a chance to get started."

"My house this afternoon?" asked Gunther.

"Good idea," Darlene said.

Casey glanced around the table and sighed. "All right," she said. "You win, Goony. This time."

10

Casey quick-stepped down 199th Street, trying to catch up with Gunther and Darlene. "Hurry, Mindy," she said over her shoulder. "If Goony gets it into his head that he can run this whole thing, my newspaper idea will be ruined."

Gunther took a shortcut across his front lawn. "Come on, gang," he yelled, climbing the steps. He leaned on the bell until his mother came to the door.

Casey was surprised to see Mrs. Reed up close. She looked like a perfectly ordinary woman. Certainly not the kind of person to have a kid like Gunther. She wondered if Mrs. Reed realized how revolting her son was, jumping around the hall with his filthy shirt hanging out all over the place.

But Mrs. Reed didn't seem to notice. She ran her hand over Gunther's head as she smiled and invited them into the living room. It was a sunny room, all yellow and green, Casey noticed. She wished her mother had as much style as Mrs. Reed.

"A newspaper?" Mrs. Reed said after Gunther told her why they were there. "What a perfectly wonderful idea."

"It was mine," Casey said. She wanted to make sure they kept everything straight right from the beginning.

Goony leered at her. "This is Casey, Mom. She's the one I told you about, the one who wants to be a celebrity."

Casey's face burned. She could hardly look at Mrs. Reed. "Well, if we're here," she mumbled, "we might as well get to work."

Mrs. Reed laughed. "Don't let him bother you, Casey. He really admires you a lot." She turned to the door and said over her shoulder, "I'll be right back with some soda."

Casey looked at Gunther curiously. He slowly crossed his eyes and stuck his finger up his nose.

She shuddered. "You're really disgusting." Then she turned her back on him and spoke to the others. "I thought if we looked at a real newspaper first, we could write down a list of things we could include in our own."

Darlene nodded. "Do you have any old newspapers, Goony?" She unzipped her schoolbag and took out a pencil and paper. "I'll make the list."

"No, that's all right," Casey answered quickly. "I have a pencil right here." She fumbled in her pocketbook. "Get the newspaper, Goony."

"Did you ever notice," he said, "that everyone wants

to be the boss around here? And nobody wants to be just a plain worker?"

"Oh, shut up and get the paper," Casey said.

He stood up and sauntered out to the hall. "Here you are, Tinsel Teeth," he yelled. The paper came sailing across the room.

Casey reached for it and handed it to Mindy. Better give her something to do, she thought. If Mindy got bored and went home, they'd lose the only plain worker they had in the whole place.

Mindy knelt on the floor and spread the paper around her. "Well," she began, "there's the news of what's going on in the world—"

"Wait a minute," Casey broke in. "How about the title first? We'd better decide on a name for ourselves."

"How about 'Fourth-Grade News'?" Mindy suggested.

"Terrible," Casey and Darlene answered at once.

Goony looked at Casey. "How about 'Gunther's Goodies'?"

Mindy giggled. Casey didn't bother to answer.

"It really has to have something like 'Telegram' or 'Herald' or 'Observer' in it," Darlene said.

"Good idea." Casey nodded approvingly. "How about 'The Ogden School Observer'?"

Darlene looked up at the ceiling, considering. Finally she began to write in her notebook. "Yes," she said. "That looks good."

"I told you I'd do the writing," Casey said.

"No harm in both doing it," Darlene answered. "Actually it's better that way. Otherwise you might lose our only copy."

Casey smoothed out her paper and wrote in large letters:

THE OGDEN SCHOOL OBSERVER

EDITED BY CASSANDRA ELEANOR VALENTINE

She held the paper in the air for Darlene to see. "Do you know how to spell my name?"

"Look here, Casey," Darlene said. "There's no need for your name to be hanging up there right on top. We're all doing the work. If you think I'm going to spend all my time writing this newspaper and not get any of the credit, you're crazy."

"I think she's right, Casey," Mindy said. "Why don't we make a box on the bottom of the first page with all our names in it. Yours can be first and say 'editor' after it."

"It was my idea—"

Gunther broke in. "I guess you've said that only about twenty-five times in the last ten minutes."

"All right." She glared at him as she crossed her name out under the title.

Mindy turned a page of the newspaper. "Don't forget about sports and recipes."

Casey wrote furiously.

"Don't forget obituaries." Gunther snickered, looking over Mindy's shoulder as she turned a page.

"What's that?" Mindy asked.

"When you die, you get to have your name in the paper," he answered.

"Keep acting like a turkey and you'll be the first one in that section," Casey said.

"I've been shot by Boss Tinsel Teeth," Gunther yelled and dropped to the floor. "Shot right in the—"

"Gunther," his mother said from the doorway, "cut that out and take this tray."

He got to his feet, took the tray of sodas from his mother, and set it down.

"Behave yourself," she said and disappeared down the hall.

"Yeah," Casey said. "Come on, be serious, *mes amis*. I'd really like to get this thing started."

Mindy nodded seriously. "It's nearly four thirty. It'll be time to go home soon."

"We can't just go home," Casey said, annoyed. "Don't you know anything about a real newspaper? Haven't you heard about deadlines?"

Gunther held up his arms. "All right. I surrender." He sank back to the floor. "What do you want me to do?"

"I guess you could be a reporter. Wander around the school and the neighborhood looking for news."

"Right," Darlene said. "Anything important that happens or anything interesting."

"Even if it happens at the last minute," Mindy said. "You know we could stop the press and add it right in."

"You mean stop the ditto machine," Casey said.

"Okay, I get it," Gunther said. "What are the rest of you going to do?"

"I'll write a society column," Darlene put in quickly. "I guess I'd be the best qualified to do that."

"All right," Casey said. She'd better not make a fuss in case Darlene changed her mind about inviting her to the birthday party. "Since I'm the editor I'll run the whole thing. Ask Walter to write something about the weather maybe. We might do something about science. Then all we have to do is put it together, write it up, learn how to use the ditto machine, and—"

"Yes," Darlene interrupted loudly. "I'll be the society reporter. Good thing my party is coming up. That's the first thing that'll go into the column."

11

"Hey, wait up," Casey yelled to Walter the next after-noon. He was halfway across the schoolyard on his way home. She shifted her books under her arm and raced to catch up with him.

"*Bonjour*," she said a little breathlessly. "Important afternoon coming up."

"Bone sur," he answered. "Why?"

"It's finally Darlene's party day. Thought it would never come. Can't wait to get home to see what my mother bought for her. I told her to get something special, something with—you know—class."

"A celebrity present?"

"You got it. Exactly."

"Why didn't you go with her?"

"Forgot about the present until this morning. Besides"—she kicked a stone out of the way—"I couldn't think of anything myself."

She waved good-bye as Walter turned up his path; then she cut across her front lawn. Throwing open the back door, she called, "Hey, anybody home here?"

Her mother appeared at the kitchen door, finger on her lips. "Ssh, Van's sleeping. She was sent home sick from school an hour ago."

"What's the matter?"

"Sore throat, I think."

"Probably just sick of school, if you ask me." Casey tossed her books on the kitchen chair. "Did you get a present for Darlene?"

Her mother nodded. "On the dining-room table. I didn't wrap it yet. Thought you might like to see it first."

Casey took a doughnut off the plate on top of the refrigerator. "What did you get?" she asked.

"A game. It was on sale at Breen's."

Casey wandered into the dining room. There was a cardboard box on the table. Written in large red letters across the yellow-and-orange box were the words: STANDOUT: A GAME FOR ALL AGES. She picked it up and listened to the pieces rattling inside. "More like a game for two-year-olds," she muttered. "I'd be laughed right out of the party if I brought something like this."

"Did you say something, Casey?" her mother called.

She cleared her throat. "I think Darlene may have this game already."

"Oh, dear." Her mother came into the dining room. "It's really too late to get anything else now. I'm sure Breen's will exchange it for her."

"I guess so," Casey said slowly. She laid the box gently on the table. "I'm going up to change."

"Try not to wake Van."

Casey went slowly up the stairs. She had about ten minutes to find a way out of this mess. Her mother was right. There was no time to buy another present. She'd have to find something of her own. But what?

She tiptoed into the bedroom and looked around. On her dresser were two stuffed animals that she had won at a carnival in August, but they seemed a little gray and dusty. Besides, she wasn't sure Darlene would be interested in a pair of lavender pandas. She opened her dresser drawer and poked around, looking at her jewelry. She held a silver bracelet up to the light but quickly dropped it back into its cotton nest. The clasp was broken and one of the stones had fallen out.

Then she spotted the necklace. It was perfect. Made of square wooden beads, it was the color of beach sand on a sunny day.

There was only one problem. The necklace was Van's. In fact, when she ran the beads through her fingers, she noticed that a brown V was stamped on the center bead. V for Van. Could just as well be V for Verona.

She turned toward the lump in the middle of Van's bed. "Vanny?"

"Mmm?"

"Can I have your brown bead necklace?"

The lump moved a little. "No."

"You never use it. It's a stupid-looking thing—old as the hills."

She ran the beads through her fingers.

"Mmm." The lump settled itself and was still.

Casey stood there, considering, not sure whether Van's "Mmm" meant yes or no. It meant yes, she decided at last. She tossed the necklace in the air with one hand and grabbed for it with the other.

She missed. The necklace clattered on the edge of the radiator and dropped behind it to the floor.

"Will you get out of here, Casey?" Van grumbled. "What a pest you are."

"Shut up, brat face," she answered good-humoredly. She grabbed the necklace and skipped back downstairs to get the wrapping paper.

She was ready in twenty minutes. Dressed in new gray slacks with Van's yellow scarf tied in a knot around her collar, she tucked two neatly wrapped packages under her arm and started down the street. Walter was sitting on his front steps, head bent over a pen and notebook.

She walked up his path. "Doing homework?"

"I'm working on the experiment book. Trying to think of something else now that the fish are gone. Maybe we could get some water, raise some mosquitoes or larvae or something."

"Too late, I think—nearly winter," she said. "Plenty of other things to do, though, now that my newspaper idea worked out. Weather observations, stuff like that." She paused. "Listen, Walt, do me a favor? Hide this in your garage." She handed him the Standout game.

"Why?"

"Don't want to hurt my mother's feelings." She sighed. "It's too late to explain now. I'm late for Dar-

lene's party. Stinky, ratty wrapping paper in our house.
Ribbon's been used fifty times. Had to look all over the
place to find one decent piece."

Walter nodded and started for the garage.

"I'll see you later," she called over her shoulder and
rushed down 200th Street. At the corner she turned
left and jaywalked across the street, dodging a car
whose driver sounded a long, angry blast on his horn.

"Yah-hoo to you, mister." She crossed her eyes and
waggled her tongue after him.

When she reached 202nd Street, she stopped to catch
her breath, then strode up Darlene's front path and
leaned on the bell. Lucky Darlene. It was the chime
kind. Loud too. She rang it again quickly so she could
listen. Eight rings: a ding, ding, dong, two deep bongs,
then up again with a dong and two dings. A celebrity-
type bell.

After a minute she stood on tiptoe to look in the
little window next to the door to see why no one was
coming. She jumped back as she heard a rush of feet
down the hall.

The door burst open. Darlene stood there with half
the fourth-grade girls in back of her. She held out her
hand for Casey's present, then turned and ran back
to her living room. Shouting and laughing, the girls
followed.

Casey raced into the house in back of them. "*Bonjour, mes amis*," she shouted. "Your president and
editor is here."

"Big deal. And what's this *bonjour* business?" Darlene asked.

61

"It happens that I'm learning French."

Linda Abel looked up from the floor, where she was leaning against the blue-and-green-striped couch. "Hey, Casey, you're lucky.

"I'll teach you if you—"

"How about we discuss that some other time?" Darlene cut in. "Right now I want to get to my presents." She reached for a package and tore the paper off in large strips.

"Gorgeous," she said, holding up a tan leather change purse. She dropped it back into its box and passed it around for the girls to admire.

Casey dug into the nut dish on the table next to her, and tossed a pile of nuts into her mouth.

Darlene peered into the next box. "Nice," she said indifferently, looking at Mindy's present. Casey leaned over to take a look. She recognized the yellow-and-orange box even before she saw the word *Standout* written across the front. One of the playing pieces fell out of the box and rolled under a chair. She noticed that Darlene didn't even bother to reach for the little green disk. She knew it. It was a crummy present.

She watched Mindy scramble under the chair, grab the piece, and drop it back into the box. Poor Mindy didn't have one ounce of style.

In no time Darlene was surrounded by a mound of wrapping paper and ribbons and opened boxes. Finally she picked up the long, narrow box that Casey had brought. She glanced at the card taped to the top of the package and tore into the blue-and-green wrapping paper. Casey pretended to be interested in a pink piggy bank that Joanne Palmer had brought.

"Gorgeous," Darlene shouted. Casey swiveled her head around to see Darlene holding up the chunky brown necklace. "Where did you get the beads," she asked, "and how did you ever string them?" She pulled the beads apart to show everyone the intricate knots between each bead while Casey sat there, stunned. Handmade!

Joanne grabbed the necklace. "How clever of you, Casey! I knew Gunther Reed was wrong about you."

"Gunther?"

"He said that Van was the only Valentine with style."

"He said that?" Casey asked, outraged.

"Don't be mad," Joanne said. She reached for the box and dropped the necklace into it. "Anybody who could make a necklace like that doesn't have to worry about having style."

Before Casey could answer, Darlene's older sister, Sue, appeared in the doorway. "Mom says the cake and ice cream are ready."

Darlene stood up and turned to Casey. "You'll have to come over tomorrow. Teach us all how to make jewelry. Maybe we could write up the directions in our newspaper. Have a handcraft column."

Casey gulped and nodded. Darlene led the way into the dining room.

12

Dear Tracy,

When I got home from Darlene's party this afternoon, I found another letter from you. You sure write a lot.

Everybody wanted to sit next to me at the party. They are so thrilled when I teach them how to say some words in French.

I bought Darlene a necklace. Her mother wanted to lock it up in a safe because she said it probably cost more than the whole house, but I said don't be silly, *ma chère*, it's nothing.

As usual, I'm very busy. We are going to have a class newspaper (my idea). Guess who is going to be the editor?

Love,
Cassandra Eleanor

13

Casey hung her raincoat on the hook and snapped the clothespin over her boots to keep them together. Usually she loved a rainy day in school. The classroom always seemed so bright and cozy when everything was dark and gloomy outside.

But what had started out to be a great day was certainly turning into a horrible mess. One of her boots had a hole in the toe so her sock was wet and clammy, and her rain hat had blown off, plastering her bangs to her forehead.

But that was the least of her troubles.

The problem was Van, or at least what Van had told her. Every time she thought about it, she couldn't make up her mind whether to giggle hysterically or just die of embarrassment.

She'd awakened early this morning before the alarm

had rung and watched the rain pelt the window. Then she stretched and looked over toward her sister's bed.

Finally Van opened her eyes.

Casey leaned up on her elbow. "How do you feel?"

"Not well enough to go to school."

"You're about as sick as . . ." She paused, then began again. "I mean that's too bad. Hey, Vanny, you know that bead necklace you gave me?"

"I thought I told you not to touch that."

"I took it. You don't mind, do you?"

"I certainly do," Van said.

"I'll give you a dollar when I get some money. But right now I need to know how to make it."

Van shrugged. "Who knows?"

"I'm not kidding." Casey slipped out of bed and began to dress. "Darlene invited me over this afternoon. I want to show her how you made it."

"Are you crazy? I didn't make that necklace."

Casey popped the last button through the hole and stared, mouth open. "What are you talking about?"

Van punched her pillow and settled back. "Listen, Casey, I'm trying to sleep. I just said I didn't string that necklace. But as long as you're going to Darlene Verona's this afternoon, ask her sister Susan."

"Why should I do that?"

"She made it for me last Christmas."

Casey stared at her sister in horror. "You big creep," she said. "You let me give that to Darlene for a birthday present?"

"You what?" Van began to laugh. "Serves you right."

Now, squaring her shoulders, Casey marched out of the classroom closet and slid into her seat just as Mrs.

Petty tapped on her desk for order. Casey tore a piece of paper out of her assignment pad, licked the point of her pencil, and began to write.

Walter:
   Urgent. Meet me in the hall *tout de suite*.
(Right away!)

C.

Nonchalantly she strolled to the corner of the room to sharpen her pencil. She dropped the note on Walter's desk as she passed. Five minutes later he signed his initials on the blackboard for the boys' room, and two minutes after that she signed hers under the girls' column. She rushed down the hall to the water fountain, where Walter was waiting.

"I'm dead, Walt," she said. "Finished."

"What's up?"

Quickly she told him about the necklace.

"You'd have been better off giving her the Standout game instead of leaving it in my garage to get greasy."

"Don't waste time about that now. What am I going to do?"

"You're dead. As you say, finished. That's the end of your celebrity life."

"Look, Walt, I don't need the jokes right now."

He leaned over the water fountain and slurped down a long drink. Then he looked up. "You'll think of something. Make up a story. You're getting pretty good at that." He wiped his mouth with the back of his hand, grinned at her, then loped back to the classroom.

For a few moments she stood looking after him.

Then she leaned down for a quick drink. She walked back slowly.

As soon as she could, she got up from her seat and went to the pencil sharpener again. This time she dropped a note on Darlene's desk.

Dear D:

What good luck you're wearing my necklace, *ma petite*. Lend it back to me so I can show the man in the store which beads I want. (They have to be ordered. They come from Bangkok.)

C.

P.S. I'll still come over today.
P.S. Again. Did your sister see the necklace?

She sharpened her pencil until it was a little stub, so that Darlene would have a chance to answer her note. On the way back she reached out and grabbed the necklace and the folded piece of paper that Darlene held out to her. Sliding back into her seat, she unfolded the paper.

C:

Tell the man to hurry up and order the beads. I didn't show my sister your necklace. I hate her guts.

D.

Mrs. Petty looked up from her desk. "You seem to have a lot of trouble getting down to business this morning, Cassandra."

Casey smiled slightly and nodded. "I'm just about ready to begin now. I hope."

14

Dear Tracy,

I received your letter when I got home from school today. I didn't get home until late because I was at Darlene's house. We were talking about our class newspaper all afternoon. It will probably turn out to be great—that is if a gross boy in my class named Gunther Reed doesn't ruin the whole thing.

It was nice of you to invite me to your house next summer. You're pretty lucky to be able to go swimming and fishing whenever you like. Do you like to eat fish? (I don't.)

Of course, I wouldn't mind sleeping in a regular-type house. In fact, it would be a nice change after sleeping in a mansion all my life. Too bad you live so far away or I'd take you up on it. Maybe when I get older.

"Dear Tracy, I received your letter."

And maybe you can visit me here. I have six bath-rooms and seven fireplaces and an in-ground swimming pool, so there's plenty of room. Maybe you can come when you're about twenty or thirty. By that time you may be able to speak French so you can talk to our downstairs maid.

Write soon, *ma chère.*

Love,
Cassandra Eleanor

15

After dismissal on Friday Mrs. Petty led the newspaper staff into the ditto room. Casey dumped her coat on top of a table and leaned against the wall with the rest of the committee. She took a long, deep breath. There was nothing in the world that smelled as good as ditto ink, unless you counted the smell of gasoline at Albano's Service Station.

She yawned, sat on the table, and swung her legs back and forth, trying to stay awake, as she listened to Mrs. Petty explain how to use the ditto machine. Teachers always seemed to repeat things over and over.

"It's very simple," Mrs. Petty said. "After you have written the article on a special type of paper called a ditto master, you are ready to begin. Turn on the machine, put your ditto master in it, set the button for the number of copies you want, then stand back. In a few minutes the copies will fall into a tray under the machine. Cassandra?"

Casey looked up.

"Suppose you tell us what to do after you have written your article on a ditto master."

Glad to be doing something besides just listening, Casey stood up and repeated swiftly, "Put the ditto master in the machine, set the button for the copies, and they'll come out on the bottom."

"You've got it." Mrs. Petty nodded approvingly.

"Not quite," Gunther said, smirking at Casey. "One little detail. She forgot to turn on the machine."

Mrs. Petty sighed. "That will do, Gunther." Then briskly she said, "Now let's get to the newspaper itself." She looked around the table. "Do all of you have your articles ready?"

Darlene pulled out a pile of papers. "I have my stuff right here." She turned to Casey. "That reminds me— did you write up the directions for the beads to put in the paper?"

Casey flushed. "Not yet."

"What beads?" Gunther asked.

"Casey gave me a necklace for my birthday. She made it herself with imported beads—from Bangkok."

Gunther rolled his eyes and grinned at Casey.

It was pretty hard to fool Gunther, she thought. "I think I'll save the directions for another issue," she said, glaring at him.

"How's your article coming, Mindy?" Mrs. Petty asked.

73

"I'm almost finished. I should be able to have it ready by tomorrow."

Mrs. Petty looked at the rest of them. They nodded.

"Well, everything seems to be coming along very nicely. You should be able to earn a good bit for the class treasury. Have you thought about how much you want to charge for each copy?"

"Not too much," Casey answered. "Otherwise no one will buy it. Maybe ten cents?"

"That sounds right," Darlene agreed. "I hope we sell a lot."

"Maybe we ought to do something to make everyone interested in buying the paper. Advertise it or something."

"We could put posters around," Mindy suggested.

"Nah," Gunther said. "Posters all over the school now. Nobody even bothers to read them."

"Even so," Mrs. Petty said, "I think you might make a few."

"I'll do that." Mindy looked around. The rest of them were glad Mindy wanted to do the work.

"How about a prize?" Casey asked. "We could sell chances and—" She paused to think. "Yes. We could sell chances for a nickel, and the winner could be announced in the first issue of the paper." She looked around. "How does that sound?"

"Not bad," Gunther said.

"Terrific," Mindy agreed.

"Yes," Mrs. Petty said. "I think you've really got an excellent idea."

"What can we use for a prize?" Darlene asked.

"We'll think of something," Casey said.

"I'm sure you will," Mrs. Petty said. "In the meantime you can practice using the ditto machine by running off an advertisement and some chances right now." She handed Casey a ruler, a pencil, and a ditto master.

Casey thought for a moment, then wrote carefully:

TAKE A CHANCE ON

A MYSTERY PRIZE

ONLY FIVE CENTS

WINNER WILL BE ANNOUNCED

IN

The Ogden School Observer

FIRST ISSUE ON SALE NEXT MONDAY

Casey held it up for everyone to see. "We can run lots of these off and put them around the school."

She took a second ditto master and divided it into boxes. In large letters she wrote: MYSTERY CHANCE. Underneath she drew a line. "We can put the person's name in here," she said, pointing to the line.

"Very nice," Mrs. Petty said. "Let's see if you can run them off now."

Slowly Casey attached the first ditto master to the machine and turned it on. In no time, copies of the advertisement lay in neat piles in front of them. Casey removed the first ditto master, attached the second, and ran off the chances.

"Well," said Mrs. Petty, "that settles that. Now don't forget to give me your articles within the next day or two so I can correct them."

Gunther raised his hand. "I've got a great idea. It

just so happens that I have a typewriter. I could type up everybody's stories."

Mrs. Petty nodded slowly. "I must say, Gunther, that it would be a nice touch to have everything typed up neatly."

Gunther went on. "I'm the roving reporter, too, you know, the one who goes around looking for current events. I have a lot to do on this paper."

Casey looked at Mindy. "Big deal," she mouthed.

Mrs. Petty clapped her hands to get their attention. "I think that does it now. Get your articles to Gunther and he can type them up over the weekend. I'll give you time off Monday to leave class and use the ditto room. Right now"—she looked at her watch—"I have to go back to the classroom for my things. You may put on your coats and dismiss yourselves. Quietly." She turned and clumped out of the room.

Gunther leaned over to Casey. "I can see the roving reporter's headlines now: 'Class President Digs Up Dead Fish for Dinner.'"

"You wouldn't dare, Goony."

"That's a chance you'll have to take." He snickered. "Read all about it in *The Ogden School Observer*."

"That really wouldn't be fair, Gunther," Darlene said, but Casey could see she was trying hard not to laugh.

Casey edged off the table and picked up her coat. "Gunther," she began, "you—"

He stared off into space. "'Casey Valentine in Love with Gunther Reed,'" he said. Then he grabbed up his coat and ran down the hall, with Casey five steps behind him.

Gunther raced down the steps.

"If I catch you, I'll kill you!" she yelled.

Gunther raced down the steps in front of the school. He nearly collided with two women who stood on the path waiting for their children. "Sorry," he called over his shoulder. "That girl is crazy about me. Keeps chasing me. Won't let me alone."

The women looked up the stairs toward Casey. She stopped running and, gritting her teeth, ducked behind the stone pillar on the top of the steps and waited. When she peeked out, Gunther had turned the corner, and the women had collected their children and were halfway down the block.

Casey went back into the school. She had something to do.

16

That night Casey dashed down the stairs ahead of Van and caught the phone on the second ring. "For me, *naturellement*," she said. She pulled the phone into the hall closet and shut the door behind her. "Is that you, Walt? Sorry your mother had to get you out of bed."

"Yeah. You'd better make it fast. She's having a fit. She wants to know what you're doing up so late anyway."

"I've been on the phone since supper, talking to people about the newspaper."

"Hey, I'm half asleep . . ."

"Stay awake a minute, will you, Walt? This is important. At the meeting this afternoon we decided to sell chances for a prize."

"That's why you had to call at eleven o'clock? You

could have told me that tomorrow. We have the whole weekend."

"Listen, Walter, if I know Darlene and Gunther, they'll try to sell chances to all the kids before I'm even out of bed in the morning." She ran her tongue over her braces. "Well, they're going to get some surprise."

"Do you really think anyone is going to buy a chance?"

"Sure. Why not? Walt, this paper just has to be a success. My whole campaign to get myself known around the school depends on it."

"A chance on what, anyway? And how much?"

"Five cents. And Darlene wanted to make the prize a necklace made of genuine beads from Bangkok."

"Wow."

"Wow is right. That reminds me, I wanted to tell you I buried that necklace in the fish can just before supper. I never want to see that thing again." She leaned back against a coat hanging on a hook. "It took about four phone calls to straighten that out. Darlene had already called Gunther and Mindy with that suggestion. Anyway, I finally persuaded them to make the first prize—Walter, are you still there? Walt? Wake up."

"Couldn't we just run through this whole thing tomorrow, Casey?"

"Yeah, sure. Just get up early. We've got a lot of things to take care of in the morning. Got to get into the school somehow."

"On Saturday? What are you—crazy?"

"Never mind that now. Just meet me out in front at

eight o'clock." Gently she put the phone back on the hook, opened the closet door, and went upstairs.

Van was practicing sit-ups in front of the window. "What are you up to now, Casey?" she asked.

"Nothing much. Walter and I are going to sell chances tomorrow."

Van yawned. "Might know it would be something crazy if you and Walter are involved in it."

"Shut up, will you?"

"Hey, Casey, what's that out in the backyard? Looks like a flashlight."

Casey leaned over her shoulder. "You're right. It is a light. Maybe it's a robber. We'd better call Daddy."

"Wait a minute. That's not in the yard. It's in the Secret Passageway. Looks like some kid with a shovel."

Casey drew in her breath sharply. "It's that peabrain, Gunther Reed. And he's trying to dig up—" She stuck her head out the window as far as she could.

"Hey," she half whispered, half shouted, "Goony Reed. I see you out there."

"What's the matter with him?" Van asked, popping her head out next to Casey. "It must be nearly eleven o'clock. What's he doing?"

"Goony, I mean it," Casey whispered as loud as she could. "In a minute I'm going to scream and everyone in the neighborhood will be out there."

"How do you know it's Goony?" Van asked.

"I know," Casey answered firmly. "There he goes now."

They watched as the dark form, bent nearly double, climbed the fence and disappeared across the school-

81

yard. A neighbor's dog started to bark, and Mrs. Moles's bedroom light went on.

"Kid's got the whole town awake," Van observed. "What a nut."

"Did he get it—I mean did he have anything in his hand besides the shovel?"

"What?"

"Never mind. I'll be right back."

"Where are you going?"

"Bathroom." She tiptoed out of the bedroom and crept down the stairs. Groping around on the hall table, she found the light and switched it on. Swiftly she opened the telephone book and ran her finger down under the R's.

"Three-five-nine-two, three-five-nine-two," she mumbled to herself as she pulled the phone into the hall closet.

She dialed, then listened impatiently to the buzzing. On the thirteenth ring someone fumbled the phone off the hook.

"Mr. Reed?" Casey asked in a deep voice.

"Who is this?"

"This is a concerned citizen."

"Wha'?" he mumbled in a voice that seemed barely awake.

"I believe your son is prowling around the neighborhood."

"Wha'?" he asked again.

Casey could hear another voice in the background. "Who is that, Roscoe?"

"Prowling around the neighborhood," Casey repeated. "With a shovel. And a flashlight."

"Who is this, anyway?"

"Don't worry. He should be getting home any minute."

Gently she put down the telephone and stood in the hall, giggling. Served the fink right if they skinned him alive. She picked at her braces. She just hoped she had surprised him before he had gotten that necklace dug up. That would be all she'd need. Stupid thing to have buried it there in the first place, she thought as she climbed the stairs.

Van poked her head out from under the blanket as Casey got into bed. "Hey, you never told me what you're going to give for a prize."

"A game. It's called Standout. Actually, Mindy gave it to Darlene for her birthday, but Darlene was generous enough to donate it to a worthy cause."

17

The sun had just appeared over the houses on 200th Street when Casey crossed the driveway between her house and Walter's. She clutched a large envelope to her chest and huddled against the side of Walter's house.

While she waited, she pried the dirt out from under her fingernails. She had spent the last ten minutes digging in the Secret Passageway. The necklace was there! She had scared Gunther away in time.

She squinted up at Walter's window and shivered. It certainly was taking him long enough to get dressed and downstairs.

Finally he appeared.

"By the time we get started, it'll be suppertime," she complained.

He held out half an English muffin dripping with butter and leaned against the house next to her. "What's this all about, anyway?" he asked. "And what's in that envelope?"

She took the muffin and licked some butter off the top. "I'll tell you all about it after we get into the school."

"You'll get us expelled yet," he said.

"We're not going to commit a crime. I just want to take care of a few things that we can't do with a million teachers and kids around to slow things down." She wiped the crumbs off her mouth. "That was good. I didn't bother with breakfast this morning. Let's go."

"How do you think we're going to get in the building? Leo, the custodian, says he locks everything up tight as a drum every night."

"Leo's lucky a real burglar doesn't want to get into the school. He'd be out of his custodian's job fast if Mr. Rosenstrauss ever found out what Leo means by locking up."

She trotted ahead of Walter across the schoolyard. "I opened the grating in the cafeteria window after dismissal yesterday afternoon. Leo was so busy rushing around sweeping up so he could get out early that he never even looked to see what I was doing."

"Will you tell me what we're going to do in there? You want me to risk my neck and I don't even know what I'm doing it for."

Casey knelt in front of the grating and folded it back against the side of the brick wall, then slid the cafeteria window open. "Let's get inside first, then I'll tell you all about it." She swung her legs over the sill and jumped down on a table. "Come on. We'll head for Mrs. Fiedler's room first."

Walter sat on a bench and shook his head. "No good."

"What do you mean?"

"I mean I'm not moving until you tell me what's going on."

She sighed. "Nothing but waste time this morning. All right." She brushed her bangs off her forehead. "We go up to the sixth grade—Mrs. Fiedler's. I heard Van say that she had a class list in her desk. All we have to do is borrow it and we've got the names and addresses of every kid in the sixth grade. Then all we have to do is go to their houses and sell them chances."

"Crazy," Walter muttered. "Why is it so important to sell chances to six-graders?"

"Can't you figure anything out, Walt? Darlene and Gunther will never think of selling to them. They'll concentrate on the fourth grade. Not only will we sell more chances this way, but I'll be able to introduce myself to everybody as Casey Valentine, the president of the fourth grade and editor of the brand-new paper *The Ogden School Observer*." She pushed open the cafeteria doors. "Everyone in the school will know me, and for the first time in my life that snooty old Van won't be ahead of me."

Reluctantly Walter followed her up the stairs. "Just a quick stop in the office, Walt," she said. "The teachers hang their keys on a rack every night. We'll pick up Mrs. Fiedler's and—"

"And?"

"Pick up the keys to the ditto room, too."

"Now what?"

"Walter, the whole day is slipping right through our fingers while you pot around making a fuss over every idea I have."

She went into the office and grabbed the keys before he had a chance to answer.

When she came out of the office, Walter waved at her wildly. She paused and looked over the edge of the staircase and out the large window on the stairs to where Walter was pointing.

"Here comes Leo with his keys." Walter whispered in a strangled voice. "He probably comes in every Saturday to make sure no one is in here."

"Hurry," she said.

They raced up the stairs to the third floor. They could hear Leo moving around downstairs, whistling while he opened a door.

They sped down the hall to the sixth-grade room. "Hold this," Casey said, handing Walter the envelope. She looked at Mrs. Fiedler's keys. There were six of them on the ring. "Nutty teachers. Always have a hundred keys when they need about two." Her hands shook as she tried one key after another. Walter jiggled up and down on his toes, watching the stairs over his shoulder. "He's coming up the stairs. Hurry!" he whispered.

Frantically Casey jammed the last key in the lock and turned it. She twisted the knob in her hand and the door opened. They tiptoed into the room and ran as quietly as they could to the closet in the back.

Hearts pounding, they crouched on the closet floor.

"You think you're so smart, Casey," Walter whispered furiously. "Think Leo is such a dope. Well, he's not so dumb after all."

"Ssh," she said. "He'll probably be gone in a minute. I see him at the park every Saturday playing tennis with some old geezer. He'll probably be gone in a minute."

For a long time they sat there. Then Casey poked her head out of the closet to listen. "Probably gone already." She tiptoed to the side of the classroom and peered out the window. "See? There he goes. I told you, Walt. Easy as pie."

"Some pie," he muttered.

She skipped over to Van's desk. "Just look at this stuff, neat as anything." She pulled out a stack of papers carefully clipped together. "Yup. Right here. Class list. We'll just take this along to the ditto room and shove the rest of the stuff back.

Walter sighed and followed her downstairs to the ditto room. "You still haven't told me—"

"Well, it just so happens that in this envelope I've been carrying around is a ditto master I wrote last night. It's supposed to be part of the class newspaper."

"What do you mean, supposed to be?"

"I'm going to run off a few copies. One or two. Then I'm going to give Tracy a little treat in her next letter."

"Tracy Matson?"

"Listen, Walter, are you supposed to be some kind of an echo? You sound like a parrot. I'm trying to explain to you. Tracy will flip when she sees this copy of *The Ogden School Observer*. She'll really think she has a celebrity for a pen pal."

Casey poked her head out of the closet.

When they reached the ditto room, Casey clipped the ditto master to the machine and pressed the button. She watched with satisfaction as the copies started to flip out of the end of the machine into a catcher, looking neat, professional, and smelling deliciously of ditto ink. She shut off the machine and held up a copy.

Suddenly Walter yelled. "Here comes Leo again. Let's get out of here."

Hastily she grabbed up the rest of the copies and raced back to the office to return Mrs. Fiedler's keys. Then she followed Walter downstairs into the cafeteria and out the window. It wasn't until they reached the schoolyard that she began to feel uneasy. Had she forgotten something? She stood there for a moment thinking. Then she shrugged and pounded out of the schoolyard gate.

18

Dear Tracy,

I'm enclosing a story that will be run in *The Ogden School Observer* this week. I know you'll be glad to hear I escaped without injury.

CASEY VALENTINE RECEIVES MEDALS FOR SAVING THE OGDEN SCHOOL FROM TREMENDOUS FIRE

The principal, Mr. Rosenstrauss, explained to the press that there was complete panic when the Ogden School furnace blew up. People ran for their lives. Mrs. Petty tried to put the fire out by spraying water through her teeth.

Casey Valentine, however, showed great courage. She carried Mrs. Petty out on her back, led the children to safety, and returned, battling smoke and fire, to grab Mrs. Crump, who was running off dittos that said, "School closed for five years because of fire."

The President of the United States made a special stop at the school to present Casey Valentine with a medal. "This young lady is really a celebrity," the President said. "When the school is rebuilt, the town should name it after this heroine."

The President also told the crowd that the President of France has invited Casey for a trip to Paris to receive the Croix de Guerre for bravery. (And also because she knows French.)

You'll be happy to know, Tracy, that instead of naming the new school for me, I suggested they call it the Walter Moles School for our dear old friend.

Love,
Cassandra Eleanor

19

Casey banged the back door shut, dropped a bag of chance stubs and money on the table, and collapsed on a kitchen chair. Van turned from the counter where she was pouring herself a glass of soda. "Where have you been all day? Mom's having a fit. It's almost suppertime and you haven't even had your lunch yet."

"Selling chances for the newspaper." Casey dug into the bag. "I took your class list out of your desk this morning. Better take it back before I lose it or something. Things like that have a way of happening to me."

"How did you get into the school? Are you crazy, going in there on a Saturday?"

"That was ages ago, early this morning. Worked out perfectly fine, *très amusant*." She shrugged out of her jacket. "How about pouring me a little of that soda instead of taking the whole bottle like a big hog?"

"I went to the store for it," Van answered mildly as she took a tall yellow glass out of the cabinet.

"Sorry," Casey said, feeling guilty. She smiled. "You should see how much money I collected, Vanny. I sold chances to half the fourth-graders and got to twenty of the twenty-three kids in your class."

"What happened to the other three?"

"Two weren't home and the third kid kept saying he didn't speak any English."

"That's Gordie Haywell. He does that to be smart."

"Sounds like an idiot, just like Goony Reed."

"Goony's not such an idiot," Van said.

Casey wiped her mouth with the back of her hand. "You must be joking. All Goony does is pester me, tease—"

"You mean like last night?"

"Exactly. Who'd want to dig up my private property in the middle of the night unless he was a complete dummy like Gunther?" She ran her tongue over her braces.

"Sometimes you're really blind, Casey," Van answered. "About yourself and everybody else."

"I can see enough to know that Goony's a pain in the A."

"That's because he likes you and doesn't know how to act."

Casey brushed her bangs off her forehead. "Likes me? That's what his mother said when I was at his house."

She picked up the bag of money and dumped it out on the table. "Likes me," she muttered to herself. "I never even thought of that. And his father probably killed him last night when he got home."

She started to count. "Over a dollar. Add that to the money the other kids will collect, and the newspaper money when we sell the paper, and we'll probably have the biggest treasury in the school."

Van swallowed the last of her soda. "You're really something. We have about forty cents in the sixth-grade treasury."

"Don't tell me I've finally done something better than Van Valentine, smartest girl in the school?"

"Is that what you think?" Van laughed. "The only reason I get such good marks is because I spend so much time studying. Practically anyone can do that."

Casey grunted. "That's what you think. And how about being such a great gymnast?"

Van leaned over and touched her toes. "Nothing to it, old girl. Everybody's good at something."

Casey clicked her teeth. "I just wish I knew what I'm good at."

They both jumped as the kitchen door banged open. Mr. Valentine stood there, juggling a roller and two cans of paint.

"This should finish up the hall," he said. He put the roller on the counter and the paint cans on the floor. "Your room is next, girls," he said. "And I hope it's the last time I have to cover up fingerprints all over the ceiling."

"I'll wash my hands before I practice from now on," Van promised. "But we still haven't decided on a color yet. Maybe dusty rose instead of blue."

"Yucky," Casey said. She stared out the window

dreamily. "If you don't want the Olympic colors, how about a nice plum color? Maybe just on two walls and the ceiling—with a light green on the third wall and—"

"That's not a paint job, that's a nightmare." Van giggled.

Casey glared at her and stood up briskly. "I have no time to worry about this painting business now, anyway. I've got to go upstairs and think about writing my article for the newspaper. It was supposed to be finished yesterday."

She blew a kiss to her father and raced up the stairs to her bedroom.

20

Casey pretended she was reading her social studies book with the rest of the class until it looked as if Mrs. Petty were falling asleep in front of the room. Then she pulled out her article. It still wasn't finished. She was late as usual; it was a good thing Goony had brought his father's typewriter to school so he could type at the last minute.

She hadn't been able to decide on something to write all weekend. By the time she had remembered to tell Walter that they were supposed to do something with weather observations, it was too late to start.

In desperation, just before bedtime Sunday night, she had glanced at the barometer her father had given her for her birthday, and decided to do an article about it. But even though it was a handy little gadget for her science experiments with Walter, writing about it was pretty dull.

She looked in the encyclopedia, changed some words around in her mind, and began to write. But halfway through the article, she had yawned and decided to finish it in the classroom Monday morning.

Now she read it over and quickly added two last sentences. Then she sat back to think about the newspaper that was coming out at lunchtime. Mrs. Petty had promised that the class could have the drawing for the prize at eleven o'clock and that the committee could go downstairs and run the paper off in the ditto room right after that. But it seemed as if the clock weren't moving at all.

She glanced over toward Gunther in the seat next to hers. She wondered if Van was right. Maybe Goony actually . . . Just then he looked up and noticed her staring at him. She smiled tentatively. In reply, he made a horrible face.

He pulled a folded piece of paper out of the back of his social studies book and tossed it on her desk. "How's this article by the roving reporter?" he whispered.

Casey glanced up at Mrs. Petty, but she was still sitting in front of the room, head bowed over the social studies book. Quietly Casey unfolded the paper. In large block letters Gunther had written across the page:

BEADS FROM BANGKOK BURIED FOREVER

Angrily she started to make a face but noticed he was grinning.

Suddenly she began to laugh.

"Did you get into much trouble the other night?" she whispered.

He shook his head. "Nah, no more than usual."

She picked up the paper. "You're not really going to—"

He grinned again. "Nah. I guess not."

Mrs. Petty looked up over her glasses. "Cassandra, will you read the last paragraph, please?"

Casey jumped. She ran her finger down the page to find the place. In a loud voice she read about the prairie and the building of the sod houses. At last, with relief, she closed the book with a bang.

Mrs. Petty looked at her watch. "It's time now to have our raffle. We'll choose the winner so the committee can print the name in this afternoon's newspaper." She looked around at the class. "I think it would be fitting for our editor to draw the name out of the box. Cassandra, will you come up here?"

"*Naturellement*," said Casey, delighted, and sailed up to the front of the room.

Mrs. Petty shook the box of chances and held it over Casey's head. Standing on tiptoe, Casey reached into the box and dug around to get to the very bottom, then pulled out a folded piece of paper.

"Who is it? Who won?" Joanne yelled.

Mrs. Petty smiled. "I guess you'll have to buy a copy of the paper to find out. Only the committee will know before the paper is distributed this afternoon." She turned to Casey. "You and the rest of the committee may put your things away now and go down to the ditto room."

Hastily Casey slid her social studies book into her desk and followed Darlene and Mindy out to the hall. Gunther trailed behind them, lugging the heavy typewriter. As soon as the classroom door closed behind them, Darlene and Mindy stopped in the middle of the hall. "Who won?" they whispered together.

Casey fished around in her pocket and pulled out the slip of paper. She unfolded it, looked down at the careful writing, and gulped. "It says," she announced, "Edith M. Petty."

"Good grief," Darlene said.

Gunther set the typewriter on the floor and waved his hand to get the circulation going again. "How did her name get in there?"

"I sold her a ticket," Casey admitted. "A nickel is a nickel. Besides, I never thought she'd win."

"I bet half the school will be mad as anything when they find out a teacher won the prize—" Mindy began.

"And blame it on the editor," Casey added glumly.

"It was a crummy prize, anyway," Darlene said.

Casey glanced at Mindy quickly. "My mother thinks it's a very good game," she said and pretended not to notice Mindy's grateful look. "Let's go, everybody, or the paper won't even be out this afternoon."

Downstairs she rattled the knob of the ditto room door. "Locked. Wait here and I'll get the key." She hurried down the hall to the office.

Mrs. Crump, the secretary, sat at her desk, typing.

Casey stood there waiting. When Mrs. Crump didn't look up, she said, "Excuse me, the ditto room is . . ."

The secretary looked up briefly, her severe brown

eyes magnified by thick, round glasses, "I'm busy. You'll have to wait."

The second hand swept around the large office clock as Casey stood there, fidgeting from one foot to the other. It was ten minutes after eleven and Gunther still had to type her article. They'd never be ready to set up their stand in front of the cafeteria by lunchtime.

Finally Mrs. Crump looked up again. "What is it, Van?" she asked irritably.

"Casey." She landed on one foot. "I'm Casey."

"Well, what do you want?"

"We're supposed to run something off on the ditto machine, but the door's locked."

Mrs. Crump scraped back her chair and scooped up a ring of keys from the corner of her desk. "Have to do everything around here," she complained as she clicked down the hall ahead of Casey. "Attendance cards to be typed, telephones ringing constantly. Now I have to be the custodian too." She twisted the key in the lock and swung the door open. "Hurry up, children. In a little while I have to use the ditto machine for an important memo for Mr. Rosenstrauss." She turned and hurried back to the office.

"Hurry, Goony," Casey said and held the door open for him.

He heaved the typewriter up on a table and flipped in a ditto master. "Give me your article," he said.

She handed him her paper, feeling a little uncomfortable. Now that she thought about it, her article really wasn't good at all.

Gunther looked at the title, "Important Facts About

"Hurry up, children," Mrs. Crump said.

Barometers." "Hmm," he said. "This seems like a really interesting and informative article."

She giggled. "Best I could think of. You know, Goony, I'm just realizing, I'm not the best writer in the world."

He looked up. "Well, you organized the whole paper. That's something, isn't it?"

She looked over his shoulder for a moment while he typed. He really wasn't the best typist in the world either, she noticed. Twice he ripped the ditto master out of the machine, crumpled the paper into a ball, and threw it on the floor.

It wasn't until eleven thirty that he typed the last sentence. At the same time, there was a click at the door. Mrs. Crump's face peered around the edge. "Are you still here? Not finished? What have you children been doing all this time?"

"We're going to run off—" Casey said.

"Too late," Mrs. Crump interrupted. "Much too late. Mr. Rosenstrauss needs his memo dittoed up right away."

"But—" Casey began.

"No buts, Van," Mrs. Crump said emphatically. "Leave your ditto masters here. If I have the time I'll run them off for you. But I doubt it very much. Go back to your classroom, and I'll send for you when they're finished."

21

There was nothing they could do but leave the ditto room. Slowly they trailed up the stairs to the classroom.

"Forty-eight posters all over this building," Casey moaned. "Every kid in the school expecting to read our newspaper at lunchtime." She shook her head. "What an old creep she is." She shoved the classroom door open.

Mrs. Petty looked at them inquiringly.

"Mrs. Crump wanted to use the ditto machine," Casey said. She watched Mrs. Petty for a moment, hoping that she might think of a way to help them.

But Mrs. Petty just shrugged. "Too bad," she said before she turned back to the blackboard.

Might have known, Casey told herself, and slammed into her seat. She slapped her notebook on the desk and began to copy her work.

By the time the clock said two minutes to twelve, she had finished most of the fill-in-the-blanks Mrs. Petty had chalked on the board. She was fishing around in her desk for her lunch bag when the door opened. Mrs. Crump stood there, lips pressed together, a pile of paper in her outstretched hands.

Casey looked at her. She couldn't believe it. It looked as if the old creep had done the newspaper for them. She watched as Mrs. Petty motioned to Joanne in the first seat to take the papers.

Mrs. Crump glared at them through her thick, round glasses. "I have the newspaper. Three pages, run off, stapled, ready to go."

Darlene looked over at Casey and held up three fingers. "Three?" she whispered. "What's she talking about?"

Casey circled her ear with her index finger. "Flipped," she mouthed. The old idiot's gone crazy, she thought to herself—the newspaper was only two pages.

"I don't know what those children were doing down there. Fooling around. Nonsense and silliness. They should have mentioned that they had already clipped one page of the paper into the ditto machine."

Casey spoke up. "We did not."

"Are you calling me a liar, young lady? Your name was right on the top of the page." Mrs. Crump turned to Mrs. Petty. "There was no sense in my taking their page out to start Mr. Rosenstrauss's work. Waste of effort. So I ran theirs off first."

Casey brushed away an uneasy feeling as she listened to Mrs. Petty thank Mrs. Crump. "I'm sure," said

Mrs. Petty, "the children are very grateful." She looked at Casey.

Darlene and Casey spoke together. "Thank you, Mrs. Crump."

As the secretary marched out of the room, Mrs. Petty tapped her hand on the desk. "Hurry," she said to the committee. "You'll have time to set your newspaper up on the table outside the cafeteria before the rest of the school comes in for lunch."

Casey tugged her lunch bag out of her desk and sped to the front of the room. She scooped up the newspapers and led the way down to the first floor.

To one side of the large double doors in front of the cafeteria was a long metal table. Together they arranged the newspapers in neat rows, glancing down at the top sheet. *The Ogden School Observer*, typed across the top, made the paper look professional, and their articles typed by Gunther with only a few cross-outs didn't look bad either.

In the center of the first page was a large box, which read:

MRS. EDITH M. PETTY

WINS PRIZE

Casey ran her finger across it. "A shame," she said. "Teachers have to get into everything around here."

Darlene took a box out of her lunch bag and held it up. "To collect our money," she said.

Casey nodded.

"Hey, Casey," Mindy asked, "what do you think Mrs. Crump meant about three pages instead of two?"

Casey started to flip to the third page, but a class marched down the stairs and across the hall toward the cafeteria doors. The front of the line stopped when the children saw the newspapers. Within a few minutes clumps of children surrounded the table, holding out money, and by the time the last class had filed by them, Darlene's cash box was full.

With five minutes left of the lunch hour, every copy was sold except for the four Casey had tucked under the table for the committee. She pulled them out and stretched. "I guess that's it, kids," she said. "Time for us to have a quick lunch."

They went through the double doors into the cafeteria just as three sixth-grade girls were coming out. They looked at her curiously. One said, "You're Casey Valentine, right?"

Casey nodded with satisfaction. Not Van's sister. Herself. Casey. They knew exactly who she was. She turned to look after them and was surprised to find that they had turned to look at her. But they were giggling.

Puzzled, Casey headed for the fourth-grade tables with Darlene and Mindy. The rest of the class had finished lunch and were in the schoolyard until the bell rang.

"I can't wait to read this over, can you?" Mindy asked them through a mouth filled with peanut butter.

Darlene nodded. "Nice of Mrs. Crump to get it ready for us. I wonder why she thought there were three pages, though, when there were only two?"

Casey flipped the newspaper open. "There are

three," she began in a surprised voice. "Look. One, two . . ." and gasped.

Almost jumping out at her on the third page were the large block letters she had printed so carefully for Tracy Matson's letter:

CASEY VALENTINE RECEIVES MEDALS FOR SAVING THE

OGDEN SCHOOL FROM TREMENDOUS FIRE

22

Suddenly it was clear to her. She knew exactly what had happened. On Saturday when Leo had come back to the school, she had grabbed up the copies she'd made for Tracy's letter but had completely forgotten the ditto master still in the machine. Mrs. Crump must have thought it was part of their paper and had run it off and stapled it right to *The Ogden School Observer*.

She stared at the newspaper. Finally she folded the paper in half, stuck it in her pocket, and swung her legs over the bench. "I've got to go to the girls' room, kids," she said in a strangled voice.

Mindy looked up from her milk. "You'd better hurry. The bell is going to ring in a few minutes and I haven't even had time to read our paper."

Casey scurried out of the cafeteria and down the hall to the girls' room. Inside, she glanced in the mirror.

Her freckles stood out like big brown blotches against her long white face, and her bangs, as usual, hung down over her eyes. She looked terrible. Maybe she could go upstairs to Mrs. Petty and tell her that she was sick—flu maybe, or a virus—and that she'd better go home right away.

Too bad it wouldn't work. She might be able to fool Mrs. Petty about being sick, but she'd never fool her mother. Mom would have her back in school in five minutes.

She banged open one of the gray metal toilet doors and bolted it behind her. Instead of spreading paper on the seat the way her mother always told her to, she sat down and took the newspaper out of her pocket. Smoothing it out on her lap, she read it carefully.

It was every bit as bad as she had expected. In fact, it was worse. The only way she could ever get out of the mess she was in was to hope that the school furnace would explode in the next two minutes and that she could personally rescue twenty-five people before the whole school read the paper. Even then she wasn't too sure that the President of the United States could be expected to be sitting around waiting to present her with a medal for bravery.

What she looked like, she thought bitterly, was a kid who wanted to be important and didn't have one thing to be important about. She caught her lip between her teeth. It was the truth. And the rest of the truth was that she was jealous of Van.

She heard the outside door of the girls' room open and peered out through the space between the door and the frame. It was Sue Verona and two other girls in the sixth grade.

She listened, face burning, as Sue asked the other girls, "Did you read the newspaper the fourth-graders did?"

One of the girls said, "Mrs. Petty won the prize."

"It wasn't such a hot prize anyway," someone said.

At that moment the bell rang. Lunch hour was over.

Casey leaned forward to hear what Sue Verona was saying as the three girls slammed out of the girls' room, laughing. She thought she'd heard something about a fire.

Casey covered her face with her hands and stayed in the booth a few minutes longer. Finally she left it and took awhile to wash her hands.

By this time, she thought, everyone would be back in their classrooms. She was right. There wasn't a soul in the hall when she came out of the girls' room. She trudged upstairs to her room. Mrs. Petty was saying, "Now that's enough talk about the newspaper. Back to work." Casey slid into her seat.

For the rest of the afternoon she sat there, hardly raising her head even when Mrs. Petty complimented the committee on a job well done.

When dismissal time came at last, Casey grabbed her sweater off the hook in the closet and hurried to the front of the line. She broke into a run as Mrs. Petty dismissed the line at the schoolyard gate, and she never stopped, even though she could hear Walter pounding after her, yelling for her to wait up.

She raced up the driveway to the Secret Passageway,

threw her books over in front of her, and climbed the fence. Out of breath, she sank down and leaned against a rock in the center of the Passageway. She tried to ignore Walter, who was coming up the driveway, still yelling for her.

He clambered over the fence and landed next to her. "Go away, will you, Walt? I need to be alone for a while."

"The Great Valentine alone? Just when you're finally a celebrity?" he asked.

"Don't be funny," she said sourly. "Everyone must think I'm some kind of an idiot."

"Why?" He started to laugh. "How did you ever think that up about carrying Mrs. Petty out on your back?"

She covered her face with her hands. "Don't talk about it. Don't say one more word. I've got to get out of here. Run away or something. If this were the old days I could skip out as a stowaway on a boat."

"Hang around doing crazy things, maybe you could be sent to reform school instead. That would get you out of here all right." He cocked his head. "Is that your mother calling you?"

She ran her tongue over her braces. "Yeah. There's no peace in the whole world." She picked up her books and stood up. "If I ever get another idea, just remind me of this awful mess."

He looked up at her, the sun glinting on his glasses. "You'll get another idea by tomorrow—or the next day at the latest." He laughed. "Don't worry, kid. Someday you'll make a million dollars with your ideas."

Casey climbed the fence. Waving halfheartedly at Walter over her shoulder, she walked up the driveway to her house.

Through the kitchen window she could see Van and her mother sitting at the table. She ducked when she saw her mother reading Van's copy of *The Ogden School Observer*. Why did Van have to go and show her mother that? She could feel tears burning her eyes.

In the kitchen her mother began to laugh. "Wonderful," she said.

"That Casey is really something," Van said. "The rest of the paper was pretty dull. But everybody thought Casey's letter was terrific. Even Mrs. Petty liked it. She stopped me on the way out and said that she wanted me to give the Standout game to Casey. She said she deserved it for being so creative."

"It's true," her mother answered. "She certainly is."

Casey stood outside on one foot. She couldn't believe it. "Creative." They all thought she had written the letter on purpose. To be funny. And Van had sounded so proud of her!

She opened the kitchen door and put her books on the table. Grinning shyly at her mother and Van, she said slowly, "I was thinking—maybe we could paint our room dusty pink, after all."

"You can do better than that." Van laughed. "How about midnight black?"

Casey squinted at the ceiling, considering. "Not bad. We could add a few touches of hot pink."

Her mother tapped *The Ogden School Observer* lightly. "Whatever you decide, Casey, I'm sure it will be original."

Casey nodded, smiling. "Listen," she said. "I've got to call Darlene. Ask her to come over. Mindy too." She picked up her books and started for the telephone. It was about time they all learned how to play Standout.

And tonight, when she had some time, she had a letter to write. It was about time she did something about Tracy Matson too.

23

Dear Tracy,

I received your letter the other day. I was happy to hear from you. There are some things I have to tell you.

First. I really am a celebrity. There's no doubt about that. Not only does everybody know my name now but I can't even go to the bathroom in school without hearing people talking about me.

But:

1. I'm not rich, just regular.
2. I know only about twenty words in French.
3. Walter is not dead anymore.
4. I just found out that my sister is not nearly the weasel I thought she was. In fact, she may turn out to be a celebrity herself, with a little help.

Love,
Casey

"Dear Tracy, I really am a celebrity."

P.S. Do you remember that horrible, icky, disgusting boy, Gunther Reed, I told you about? I just noticed that he's the best-looking boy in the class. (After Walter, of course.) In fact, he'll be a lot of fun when he stops trying to impress everybody in the whole world.

A YEARLING BOOK

Illustrated by Leslie Morrill

PATRICIA REILLY GIFF

THE GIRL WHO KNEW IT ALL

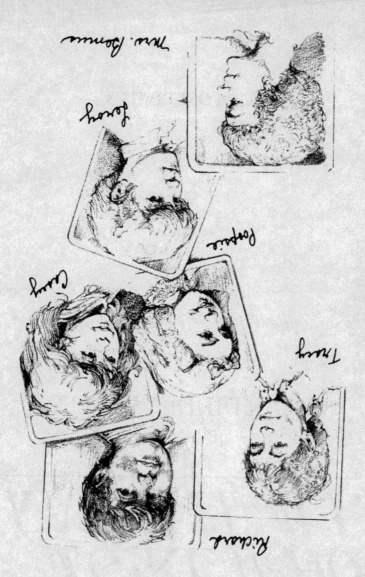

For my husband,
Jim,
with love

1

"First again," Tracy said to Herbie, the bus driver. She slid into the seat behind him, still talking. "Took me so long to get packed up for the vacation and say good-bye to my teacher I thought I'd never be first in line."

Herbie didn't answer. He was busy watching the rest of the children climb into the bus.

"Yes, sir," she said a little louder. "I guess you'd be disappointed if I didn't sit here and help you with the traffic."

"Sit back, Tracy," Herbie said. He started the engine.

Tracy craned her neck around: "You're all right on this side, Herbie. Go ahead." She leaned forward as he pulled out of the schoolyard. "We should be at High Flats by three-thirty—if you step on the gas a little."

"You know I can't do that, Tracy." Herbie looked at her in the rearview mirror. "I told you that yesterday —and the day before yesterday too."

"Sorry, I forgot. Check that car at the intersection, on your left."

"Why don't you relax, Tracy? I've been driving this bus for as many years as you have freckles. And that's a lot." Herbie laughed.

Tracy sat back, a little hurt. She didn't like to be reminded of her freckles. It wouldn't be so bad if they were the brown dot kind like everyone else's. But hers were big, and red like her hair. Once she had measured a freckle on her arm. It was bigger than the eraser on the end of her pencil.

And once Leroy Wilson had called her Fungus Face. But only once. She grinned to herself. Boy, did she fix him that time!

But today she wasn't going to think about fighting with Leroy. She was going to figure out how to become Leroy's friend, because if she didn't, she was going to spend the summer playing with that six-year-old baby, Poopsie Pomerantz.

That was the trouble with High Flats. It was probably the smallest town in the whole round world. She couldn't figure out why anybody would call it a town anyway. Mrs. Grant's living room was the post office, and there wasn't even a store or a second street. There was only High Flats Road, which started at the bottom of Hubbell Mountain and ended at the river. In between there were fourteen houses, seven on each side of the road. Tracy's was stuck on the end closest to the river, next to Mrs. Grant's. It was a brown wooden house with a skinny porch tacked on the front.

And except for Tracy, there were no girls in High Flats, unless you counted Poopsie Pomerantz. Every summer Tracy hoped that Mrs. Clausson, who had

boarders in the summertime, would get a nice girl to stay with her. But it never seemed to happen that way. Instead there were only fat ladies, old men, and sometimes boys.

Just her luck, Tracy thought, to be born in a town where there was nobody her age to play with except that idiot, Leroy, who was carrying on in the back of the bus. As usual, he was making enough noise to give everyone a headache.

That Leroy! He never wanted to play with girls. And it certainly didn't help that he was the smartest kid in the class and she was probably the dumbest—at least in reading. She'd just have to show him that she knew everything when it came to catching fish.

Tracy jumped. She realized Herbie was talking to her. "What did you say?"

"Are you falling asleep back there, Tracy? I asked how you made out on your report card."

"Could have been worse, I guess," she replied as casually as she could. She pretended she was too busy gathering up her books and gym sneakers to answer any more questions about her marks. She kept quiet and looked out the window during the rest of the trip.

Finally the bus slowed down and stopped. With a wave to Herbie, Tracy climbed out of the bus and dashed up High Flats Road ahead of Leroy.

She slowed down as she passed the empty house that used to belong to the Stewarts. It was still closed up. Next to it was Mrs. Clausson's boardinghouse. Two old men sat there, rocking on the porch, sound asleep.

Then came Mrs. Grant's house. And across the street from Grants, just before Leroy's house, lived the Schaefers. Three-year-old Bobby Schaefer stood in his

living room looking out the screen door at her. She waved and turned in at her front path.

She could hear her dog, Rebel, scrabbling behind the door. She reached for the key that dangled around her neck and let herself in.

"Just let me get rid of this junk," she told the dog. But Rebel, wiggling his bristly black tail, jumped on her till she dumped her books on the hall table and sank down next to him on the floor.

She threw her arms around him and squinched her eyes shut as he licked her face. "Boy, I'm glad you're here," she said. "I'd hate to come home without anyone to say hello to." She squeezed him hard. "Just think. It's summer vacation."

She stood up and, with Rebel trailing after her, went into the kitchen. From the window she could see Leroy already jumping around on the steel bridge that crossed the wide blue river. "Kid always needs a haircut," she said, looking at his blond hair waving in the breeze. Then she clicked her teeth in annoyance as she spotted Richard on the bridge with Leroy. He was bent over his bicycle, fiddling with it, as usual. He must have raced the school bus to get there so fast from Windsor.

She watched Leroy cast his fishing line into the water. "I better go up there and try to make friends with him again," she said to herself. "If I wait too long, the summer will be half over."

She climbed on the wooden counter to reach the cabinet above the refrigerator and knelt, shifting boxes until she found the jar she was looking for. Then she hopped down and began to make a snack. She hummed as she clattered around the yellow kitchen, opening

and shutting drawers. Finally she wiped her hands on the front of her dungarees and skipped out the back door and up the road to the bridge.

"Hey, you guys," she shouted. She balanced a brown paper bag in one hand and her tackle box and fishing pole in the other. "What are you doing?"

Leroy looked up. "Fishing, noseybody."

"I'm coming up to fish too."

"No girls," Leroy said. He shoved some hair off his forehead. "Just get out of here and play with your dolls or something."

By this time Tracy had her feet planted on the bridge. "I have a snack," she said and waved the paper bag.

Richard smacked his thick lips, hiding his broken front tooth for a moment. "Let her stay," he said, eyeing the bag.

"Well, all right," Leroy answered. "What've you got there?"

Tracy danced away from him. "We'll eat in a little while," she said, "after I show you how an expert catches fish."

She wiggled herself between the crossbars of the bridge and dangled her legs over the side, pretending that she didn't see the boys making faces at her. "I have a really terrific lure. Probably the best one around here," she said. "It was my father's, but he said I could have it."

"Good thing you got it already. After your father sees your report card tonight—" Leroy broke off and shook his head. "I wouldn't be you for a million dollars."

Richard looked up from his bike and snickered,

"No girls," Leroy said.

showing his broken tooth. "You think her father will be surprised? I guess he's used to it by now."

"Did you ever use a toothbrush in your whole life?" Tracy asked. She glared at him for a moment, then cast her line over the side of the bridge.

"What was the name of that reading group you were in?" Richard pretended to think. "Oh, yeah. The Chickadees. Slowest reading group in the world." He and Leroy flapped their arms and began to chirp. "Peep, peep." Then they laughed.

Out of the corner of her eye, Tracy looked at Leroy hopping up and down. His pole, propped against the bridge rail, began to slide. Calmly Tracy watched it fall through the crossbars.

"Leroy," she said, "your pole just fell off the bridge. But that's all right, because you don't know how to fish anyway."

As Leroy raced off the bridge and down to the rocks to get his pole, Tracy leaned against the crossbars, watching her fishing line drift gently in the water below. Leroy certainly was a difficult boy, she thought. For two cents she'd leave him flat and eat the snack by herself. But then, she reminded herself, she'd be stuck with Poopsie Pomerantz for the rest of the summer.

As Leroy panted back up onto the bridge, Tracy felt a wiggle on her line. Can't leave now, she thought with satisfaction. I'll probably catch a big one.

She raised her pole a few inches until she felt a jerk. The pole bent double.

"Told you I'd get one," she said over her shoulder and started to reel in.

Leroy leaned over the edge of the bridge to watch.

"A sucker," he said as the fish broke water. "Just a junk fish. Can't eat him." He tossed the hair out of his eyes and baited his hook. "Know-it-all," he said.

"You've lived here for just six months," Tracy said. "Don't try to act like an expert. Watch me for a while. You might learn something about fishing."

She continued to reel in as hard as she could. A sucker might be no good to eat, but a catch was a catch.

Halfway up, the fish arched its silvery body, snapped the line, and splashed back into the water.

Tracy stared at the broken line. "There goes my best lure," she said. She turned her head against the bridge so the boys wouldn't see her blink back the tears in her eyes. Then she got to her feet.

"I guess it's time for our snack," she said and reached for the bag.

Leroy looked at her. "Now you're talking. What've you got there anyway?"

Richard held out his hand.

"Icing sandwiches." She passed out two wrapped in waxed paper and kept a third for herself.

"A little stuck, I see," she said, peeling the paper off.

"Mmm, good." Leroy didn't bother to unwrap his. He kept wiggling his finger under the paper and scooping up icing so he could lick it off. When there was hardly any left, he asked, "What kind of cake is underneath?"

"No cake," Tracy mumbled, her mouth full. "I couldn't find anything in the kitchen but some stale rye bread."

"You put chocolate icing on stale rye bread?" Leroy turned to Richard. "She's crazy. I knew I shouldn't

have let her up here." He flung the bag over the side
of the bridge.

Richard took one last scoop of icing and threw the
bread after Leroy's.

Tracy watched the waxed paper and bread bobble
on the water. "That's very bad for the ecology, Leroy.
And you wasted that bread. It was the last of the loaf.
I'll bet my mother wanted it for toast."

"Then you shouldn't have smeared it with all that
icing and brought it up here. Get off the bridge now
before I throw you and your tackle box over the side."

Tracy stood there for a minute, watching Richard
lick the chocolate off his fat mouth. It was no use, she
thought at last. As long as the two boys were together,
she'd never be able to make friends. She gathered up
her gear and marched off the bridge. Leroy and
Richard flapped their arms and peeped.

"It's time for me to set the table for supper," she said
over her shoulder. "My mother will be home from
work soon."

2

Tracy left her fishing pole and tackle box on the back steps and banged the screen door after her as hard as she could.

"That boy is impossible," she said to Rebel.

Rebel rolled his large eyes at Tracy and thumped his bristly tail uncertainly on the kitchen floor.

"Do you think I'm mad at you? I'm sorry." She made her voice as syrupy as possible so that Rebel would know it wasn't his fault that Tracy seemed cross. She reached into the cabinet for a dog biscuit just in case Rebel's feelings were hurt.

"I get so annoyed with that Leroy Wilson," she said as Rebel munched contentedly on the biscuit. "Whenever I want to be his friend, everything gets twisted like a pretzel."

She slid three dinner plates off the shelf and marched to the table.

"If I try to be interested in what he's doing, he thinks I'm a noseybody." She slammed down a plate at her father's place.

"And he never stops talking about my reading." Bang went her mother's plate.

"That whole reading thing is going out of style. Waste my whole life learning to read, and by the time I grow up everybody will probably take a little green pill or something and end up knowing about the whole round world."

As she slid her plate on the table between her mother's and father's, she bit her lip. Upstairs in the bottom drawer of her dresser she had hidden her report card under a pile of pajamas. It was bad enough that she had gotten an F in reading, but Mrs. Graham had written a note in large letters on the bottom of the card:

TRACY MUST PRACTICE READING EVERY DAY THIS
SUMMER OR SHE'LL PROBABLY BE LEFT
BACK NEXT YEAR.

When her father took a look at that, he'd set up some dopey schedule, and the next thing she knew she'd be stuck somewhere reading a stupid book while the rest of the world was out fishing.

She wouldn't forget that mean Mrs. Graham as long as she lived. She closed her eyes and pictured herself grown-up and beautiful. Mrs. Graham was begging for tickets to her TV show.

"Tracy," she'd say, "I'm sorry I was cruel to you when you were a little girl."

Before she could decide if she'd let Mrs. Graham have tickets to the show, she heard her mother's car in the driveway.

Quickly Tracy scooped knives and forks from the drawer and slapped them on the table next to the plates. Then she put away the box of dog biscuits. It wasn't a good idea to let Mother know she'd been giving Rebel a snack. Dr. Wayne, the veterinarian, always complained that Rebel was too fat.

Tracy glanced at the table to make sure she hadn't forgotten anything as her mother breezed into the kitchen and dropped grocery bags on the counter.

"Whew, it's hot," her mother said. She sank down on a bench and smoothed her hair down with her hands.

Tracy loved to look at her mother's hair. It was red like hers, but a little darker and not so curly. Her mother was really pretty. She didn't have one freckle, and she had the prettiest blue eyes.

Tracy leaned over and kissed her. "How many boxes did you pack today?" she asked after her mother had hugged her back.

Tracy's mother worked for a company that shipped packages of vitamins all over the world. Tracy liked to keep score on the number of boxes her mother wrapped every day. On good days she could wrap as many as a hundred and fifty. On bad days she wrapped about seventy-five.

"About a hundred—a medium day." Her mother smiled. "I'll bet you're glad this was the last day of school."

Tracy nodded. She tried to look cheerful, but her

lips felt peculiar. It was hard to keep them from trembling.

Her mother cocked her head. "What is it, honey?"

Tracy picked at a scab on her elbow. "I lost my best lure today. Sucker. Took half the line with it."

Her mother sat still. "That happens."

"Yes," Tracy said. She cleared her throat. "Everybody thinks I don't do one thing right."

"Oh, Tracy. You do so many things right."

"I know," Tracy said. "I tell that to people sometimes. But no one believes me."

Tracy's mother laughed. "Who is everybody?" she asked. "Leroy?"

"Almost."

"And Richard?"

"That fat idiot. He doesn't count. I just wish he'd stay on the other side of the mountain in Windsor where he belongs."

"And?"

"And Mrs. Graham, I guess."

Her mother sighed. "Speaking of Mrs. Graham, you'd better let me see your report card."

"Daddy's home," Tracy said, hearing a car door slam. She ran to the back door to meet him.

"How's my number-one girl?" he asked, grinning down at her.

Tracy threw her arms around him and buried her head in his waist. "I'm glad you're home," she said in a muffled voice.

"Me too," he answered. He patted her head with his large hands that were hard and rough from working as a carpenter.

Tracy's mother leaned over to kiss him.

"Hey!" Tracy wiggled out from underneath. "I'm getting squished."

Tracy bustled around the kitchen, helping with the supper. While her mother shaped thick pink hamburgers from the chopped meat, Tracy shredded lettuce for the salad, and her father told them about the house he was helping to build in Handon, twenty miles away.

It wasn't until supper was over that her mother remembered the report card. Tracy pushed back her chair and went to get it. Holding it upside down so she wouldn't have to look at it, she handed it to her father. Then she squeezed detergent into the sink and blasted the water on top of the dishes.

"This report card is terrible," he said over the noise of the water. "You'll have to practice reading every day so you catch up by September."

She nodded.

"Fifteen minutes every morning. You've got to learn how to read well if you want to get anywhere in life. I've told you that before."

Tracy watched the white froth bubbling and rolling on the surface of the water. She thought about not getting anywhere in life. But then she shrugged. If she had her own television show, she'd just hire some smart aleck like Leroy to read everything for her.

Besides, she read enough to get by. After all, she had managed to read all of her pen pal's letters by herself—well, almost all—without asking her mother to help. And that reminded her, she hadn't had a letter from Casey Valentine in about two weeks. And the last

"This report card is terrible."

letter had been full of hints about a surprise that Casey had for her. Tracy wondered what it could be.

"Tracy," her father said sternly. "Are you listening to me?"

"Fifteen minutes every day for reading," she answered, still wondering what the surprise from Casey Valentine was going to be.

3

An orange sun shone through the leaves of the sugar maple into Tracy's window. She dug her head deep into the pillow and groaned. Had she finished all her homework last night? She couldn't remember.

A second later her head popped up. It was Monday morning and summer vacation. She had forgotten. The sheets flew off the bed as she bounded to the floor. She threw on a bathrobe and dashed downstairs and out of the house to check the mailbox.

But the red flag on the box was down. No mail again. She clicked her teeth in disappointment. What was the matter with that Casey Valentine anyway?

She turned to go back into the house.

"Hey, Tracy. Wait up," a voice called behind her.

Tracy stiffened. It was that gross Poopsie Pomerantz, dancing her way up the street. She thought she was a

ballerina just because she took ballet lessons a thousand times a week.

"Can't stop now, Poopsie," Tracy said. "I have to get dressed."

"Wait a minute, Tracy. I want to show you my new step." Poopsie stopped in the middle of the street, put one arm over her head, and twirled around three times. Then, slightly off balance, she stopped. "How was that, Trace? What do you think?"

"Actually . . ." Tracy began, "it needs some practice. Right now. . . ."

"That's right," Poopsie said. "Needs a little work. My teacher says so too. But she says nobody has to be perfect all the time either. Just do your best."

"I really don't have time to spend here all day, Poopsie," Tracy said. "I haven't had my breakfast or anything. You keep practicing. I'll see you later."

Tracy went into the house and upstairs to her bedroom. That Poopsie was a pest, she thought. Yak, yak all day. Then she giggled. Poopsie's teacher certainly was right when she said that Poopsie wasn't perfect.

She wandered over to her dresser. A note was taped to the mirror. She read it, slowly sounding out the words.

> Dear Tracy,
>   Please clean your room today. It's a disgrace. And Dad said you're supposed to read fifteen minutes every day.
>   Call me at work if you need me.
>
>   Love,
>   Mom

"Just do your best," Poopsie said.

Tracy clicked her tongue against her teeth. "Read, read, read," she said to Rebel, who was curled up on a pile of her underwear. "How can I be expected to read for fifteen minutes? There isn't even a decent book in the house."

She thumbed through a pile of birthday books from Aunt Rita. "Does she really think I'd like *The History of Asia for Young People*?" She slapped the cover so hard with the palm of her hand that Rebel jumped.

"And look at this one," she said, reaching the bottom of the pile. She sounded out *Inventions of the Greeks*. "I probably know about four words in the whole thing."

She yawned and stretched. "I know what I'll do. I'll take myself to the library tomorrow. They may have something I can get my teeth right into. Then I can add today's fifteen minutes to tomorrow's."

After all, Mrs. Graham had told her a thousand times that her only problem with reading was that she didn't read often enough. "If you read more, Tracy," she'd said, "you wouldn't make all those silly mistakes like reading 'nose' for 'noise.'"

Yes, that's what she'd do. Maybe she'd even read a little more than half an hour. Tomorrow.

She found a clean pair of old shorts and pulled a green shirt over her head. On the front of the shirt was a picture of a skunk. Underneath the skunk it said: "Be nice to me or else."

After she stuffed her nightgown under the pillow, she smoothed the bedspread over the blankets. She sighed when she noticed her sheet still on the floor instead of tucked neatly under her blanket on the bed.

"I'll fix this mess later," she said to herself and gave the sheet a halfhearted kick.

Slinging her binoculars over her shoulder, she galloped down the stairs two at a time. She grabbed a couple of doughnuts from the breadbox in the kitchen and went outside. Already the front steps were hot from the sun. She sat down carefully so the backs of her legs didn't touch the stone.

Leroy stood in front of his house across the street. He was swinging a tree branch through the tall grass.

"Hi, Leroy," she called. "Would you like a doughnut?"

Leroy clutched his throat, made a few gagging noises, and staggered around in the grass. "She wants to poison me." He groaned and fell on the ground.

Tracy took a bite of her doughnut and licked the sugar off her fingers. Then, raising the binoculars to her eyes and squinting a little to avoid the crack in one lens, she focused on Leroy.

He raised his head. "Are you still using those silly binoculars?" he yelled. "You can see just as well without them."

Tracy didn't bother to answer, so he went back to swinging the branch through the grass.

She listened to the swish-swish noise he was making as long as she could stand it. Then she lowered the binoculars and trotted back into the house to straighten her bedroom.

"This is a waste of time," she grumbled to Rebel, who was still dozing on her underwear.

"May as well start out right," she said. She pulled out the top drawer of her dresser and turned it upside down on the floor. "I'll throw about a thousand things

out and then I can put all the stuff that's on the chair
into the drawer."

She cleared a space in the center of the floor, then sat
down and began rifling through a pile of papers.
"Yucks," she said. A wad of chewing gum was stuck
to two pages of homework from last winter. She pulled
the papers apart gently, stretching the gum into a long
pink string.

Outside, a car went by. She got to her feet and
ambled over to the window to see where it was going.

"It's not a car," she told Rebel. "It's a truck. It's
stopping in front of the empty house down the street.
Wonder what it's doing there."

She opened the screen and stuck her head out to get
a better look.

Two men got out of a gray panel truck and went up
the path of the vacant house. They walked around for a
few minutes. Then one of the men went back to the
truck and pulled out a ladder and some cans of paint.

About time they painted that old place, Tracy
thought. I hope it's a decent color. It's a shame the
way people keep sticking brown all over everything in
this town.

Suddenly she pulled her head inside the window
and slammed the screen shut.

"Get out of the way, Rebel," she said. She stepped
over the dog. "I've got to see what's going on."

She raced down the stairs and out the front door.
Leroy was still standing in front of his house.

"What's going on over there?" she yelled.

"Looks like they're going to paint that house." He
followed her down the street.

"I can see that," she said over her shoulder. "I'm not blind."

"Well, you asked."

"Let's go watch," she said.

Halfway down the street, they leaned against the side of the panel truck. One of the men was scraping the side of the house. It made a screechy noise.

"Hey, mister," Tracy called. "Why are you painting that house?"

The screeching noise stopped. The man looked at Tracy and Leroy. "Get away from that truck, kids. Go on."

Tracy stopped leaning and stood up straight. "I just want to know why you're fixing that house. Is someone moving in?"

The man didn't answer. He turned around to work on the house again.

Then the second man came around from the back of the house. He looked a little more friendly.

"Mister," Tracy called. "Is someone moving in?"

The man pushed his cap back from his face. "Yup," he said.

"How long is it going to take you to paint the house?" Leroy asked.

Tracy gritted her teeth. "Wait a minute, Leroy. That's not the main thing we have to find out." She turned back to the man. "Do they have any kids?"

"What?"

"Kids," Tracy yelled. "Kids."

He shrugged. "Don't know. Just a man and his wife, I think."

"The old Tracy luck again," she grumbled. "They're

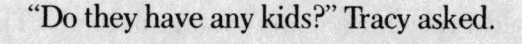

"Do they have any kids?" Tracy asked.

probably four hundred years old and wrinkled like a pair of prunes."

Leroy snickered.

"Hey, Leroy, what do you say we go fishing?"

He scratched his head. "W-ell, I don't know. Here comes Richard." Leroy shuffled his feet a little. "I have to see what he wants to do."

She watched Richard riding down the road toward them on his bike. She tried to think as fast as she could. How could she persuade Leroy to stay and play with her? She had an idea.

"I have the best fishing rod in High Flats. You know that, Leroy," she said. But before she could offer to lend it to him, Leroy glared at her.

"Sure, Tracy, sure. You have everything and you know everything. Isn't it strange that you're still the dumbest kid in the whole state?"

Richard slid to a stop. He straddled his bicycle on the edge of the curb. "How about some fishing, Leroy?" He glanced toward Tracy. "Got any snacks today?"

Leroy boosted himself on Richard's handlebars and they skidded off in the direction of the river.

Tracy stood watching the bicycle wobble away from her. "Someday I'm going to get you, Leroy," she whispered. "And you too, Richard."

4

It was a hot gray day. Clouds hung over the mountain like smoke from a campfire.

Tracy had nothing to do.

On Tuesday she had taken a book from the library. But she left it out in the rain on Wednesday. Now it was drying on the back porch. No, this was not a reading day.

Instead she wandered down the street with Rebel to look at the empty house. The painters had finished, and she had heard that the new people were moving in today or tomorrow.

"Blah," she said. The painters had started out all right with a fresh coat of white paint. The trouble was that they had painted the whole thing white. Now the house looked like a big white shoe box with a couple of holes cut out for windows.

It was plain, much too plain. She walked up the front path and stood on the steps. "Not a top-quality job at

all," she said to Rebel, who sat on the path scratching his stomach with his back paw.

She leaned over and looked at the door. "I notice there are a few drips too," she muttered and scratched at a small white lump.

Maybe there was something she could do about it. Good thing her father was a carpenter. She had heard him say that turpentine was good for thinning out lumps. "I'll just smooth this out with a little turpentine and add some more white paint," she said.

A few minutes later she stood in front of her own garage. Her father had so much equipment he couldn't even squeeze the car in anymore. The garage was filled with old rope and nails, ladders, and boxes of tools. It smelled of paint and grease.

She puttered around, looking for some turpentine and a can of white paint. "Must be forty-nine cans of paint in here," she said as she stepped over a can and studied the label. "Looks like it says 'Chocolate Brown House Tint.'"

"Turpentine . . . turpentine . . . should be in a square can, I think." She dragged a stool over to a shelf and hopped up. "Here it is," she said after she had looked at several cans. "Not a square can at all. No wonder it took so long." She pulled the heavy can off the shelf and, wobbling a little, climbed down.

In another minute she had found some white paint. Then she wiped the cobwebs out of her old wagon and piled everything into it.

Pulling the creaking wagon behind her, she returned to the empty house. "This pile of evergreen bushes in front is a big help," she said to Rebel, who had followed her back down the street. "The neighbors

don't have to know everything that's going on around here."

She dragged the wagon behind the bushes close to the house and struggled to open the can of turpentine. Humming softly, she managed to poke a stick under the lid and pry it off. "Strange," she said, looking at the thick liquid, "the label says turpentine. But this looks reddish." She shrugged. "Probably supposed to look this way."

She looked up at the shutters. "I'll do them too."

She stood in the wagon so she could reach the shutters, dipped the brush into the can, and spread it carefully on the middle of the shutter. It seemed to leave a bright pinkish-red mark. "Probably dry off clear," she mumbled. But what were those little spots? She dug at some sandy grains with her fingers, leaving smudge marks.

"The brush," she muttered, pulling the bristles apart. "Full of cobwebs and gook."

She looked around for something to wipe the brush on, but the only thing she saw was the wagon. She brushed on a large pink T and an even larger M.

Now the brush looked much cleaner. She'd just go over the part she had finished to cover the dirt spots. She dipped the brush into the can again and was surprised to see that the deeper she plunged the brush in, the redder the turpentine looked.

She brushed a little more turpentine on the shutter, then started on the door. When she'd finished, she stepped back to see how it looked. Some sections were pink, others were red, and some were half red and half pink. She rubbed her hands on her shorts nervously.

She probably shouldn't have started the whole thing.

Looking down, she noticed drops on the steps. She scrubbed at them with the toe of her sneaker, and they smeared a little.

She stared at the door and felt a terrible lump in her chest. Something was wrong. The turpentine was not drying clear; it was beginning to look redder and redder. She walked over to the wagon and looked carefully at the can of turpentine. Then she traced the letters on the front: "Tur—" she said. "Turkey Red." Her heart began to beat faster.

She rubbed her hands together. She'd have to do something about this mess, and fast. She looked at the house again. The red paint on the shutter looked a little like a fat red rose. What she needed was a can of green paint.

She raced home. Luckily there was a small can in the corner of the garage. She carried it back to the empty house.

When she opened the can, it was nearly dry. She poked her finger in it. There'd be enough for a few stems.

Standing in the wagon, she made some bright red squiggly circles on the rest of the shutters. Then, smearing green paint on her fingers, she drew green leaves and stems underneath the flowers.

She was so engrossed in her painting that she didn't hear the sound of the car coming up the driveway. But when she heard a car door slam, she hopped out of the wagon and ducked around the side of the house.

Footsteps crunched on the gravel driveway. Tracy peeked around the edge of the house.

Something was wrong.

A man and a woman walked up the path toward the front door. They were really not very old, but they weren't young either. The lady had dark hair with a streak of gray in the front, and the man was bald.

Halfway up the path, the woman stopped. "Good grief!" she said. "What happened?"

Her husband shook his head. "This is the work of lunatics," he muttered.

Tracy scrunched her head down between her shoulders. Suppose they called the police. They'd put her in jail for at least twenty years. Leroy, grown up, with a long blond beard and mustache, would still be laughing when they finally let her out.

But her mother and father wouldn't laugh. They'd have to pay for the house to be repainted. It would probably cost a hundred dollars. And they'd be so mad they wouldn't even visit her in jail.

As quietly as she could, she tiptoed toward the back of the house, through the Claussons' and Grants' backyards. She banged open the screen door, dashed up the stairs to her bedroom, and threw herself on the bed.

Even there she didn't feel safe. Trembling, she slid off the bed and opened the closet door. Inside, it was dark and smelled of rainy days, boots, and dust.

She curled up on a bunch of clothes on the floor. How glad she was that she hadn't put the clothes in the hamper. She sniffled and wiped her nose on a pair of pajamas.

Suddenly she remembered Rebel. The poor dog must be wandering around on High Flats Road looking for Tracy. Rebel didn't like being left outside alone.

Tracy crept out of the closet and down the stairs.

She peeked out the back door. Rebel was nowhere in sight. She opened the door, and called him softly, keeping her head hidden so no one would see her. Finally Rebel appeared, padding his way around the side of the house.

Tracy held the door open. Taking his time, Rebel lumbered up the three back steps and into the house. She heaved him up in her arms and raced up the stairs again and into the closet.

For a long time she sat there in the hot darkness with the dog on her lap. She began to think her mother was right. Rebel really was too fat. Tracy felt as if an elephant were asleep on top of her.

Finally she couldn't stand it in that hot closet one more minute. She opened the closet door cautiously and tiptoed to the window. She wasn't sure what she expected to see, but at the very least, she thought, the black-and-white car of the state police would be parked in front of the empty house.

Everything was quiet on High Flats Road. Faintly she could hear Leroy bouncing a basketball on the side of his house. And Mrs. Grant had the radio on. She was listening to the opera again.

"Everything seems to be just the same down there, Rebel," she said. "I guess we can risk a little snack or something. It must be past lunchtime by now. We must have been in that closet about fifty hours."

On the way downstairs she stopped short. "Wait a minute," she whispered. "Maybe no one knows that old Tracy Matson painted that house. Maybe they think it was the work of some lunatic, like the bald man said."

She took a deep breath. Maybe she was safe.

Then her heart flopped over. She remembered the red wagon with the huge pink initials T. M. painted on the side.

Her last chance to escape was gone. She'd never be able to get that wagon away from the empty house.

5

For a long time Tracy stood in the kitchen, staring out the back window. It seemed there was always something to worry about.

Finally she shook herself and reached for a loaf of rye bread.

"No sense in starving to death just because I might be in jail tonight," she told Rebel, putting two pieces of bread into the toaster.

When the bread popped up, she sliced a banana on each one. "I'll sprinkle a little sugar on these, Rebel, and then we'll eat. Something to stick to our ribs, as they say on television."

She put one slice next to Rebel's water dish and sat down with the other at the kitchen table. Thoughtfully she added another tablespoon of sugar to her banana. There must be a way out of this.

Maybe she could fool the new people.

Suppose she stopped in there later on and met them. She could say, "Did you ever meet Tommy Martin? He used to live here in High Flats. He was a lunatic, you know. Always painting people's houses." Then she'd glance up at their house and cluck her teeth sympathetically. "I see he got your house before they put him away."

No, that would never work. She couldn't lie like that. Sooner or later someone would tell the new people that Tracy Matson was the only person in High Flats who had the initials T. M.

Besides, if she tried to fool them, she'd be so scared that her hands would shake and her lips would get all funny the way they did in school when she had to read for Mrs. Graham.

She'd just have to sneak that wagon out from behind the bushes and hide it. She'd walk past the empty house right now and see what was happening.

After all, the state police hadn't come yet. If she heard sirens, she'd still have enough time to race back home and hide in the closet.

Slowly she started down her front path. She tried to whistle, but her mouth was too dry. Instead she hummed loudly.

"Wait up, Tracy," a voice called in back of her.

Tracy stiffened. Nothing ever went right. Now it was that gross Poopsie Pomerantz, sniffling and snorting from her allergies. And as usual, she had no handkerchief.

"Go away, Poopsie. Please."

"What are you doing, Tracy?" Poopsie said in a clogged voice.

"Go away, I said. I have business. It's personal."

Poopsie stepped back. "How come I can't come with you, huh? Tracy?"

"You can't. Not with that cruddy nose." Poopsie certainly was enough to turn a person's stomach, she thought.

"If I go back to get a handkerchief, you'll be gone and I won't be able to find you."

"That's the idea," she muttered.

"I'm coming with you."

Tracy could have screamed. If she stayed there arguing with that ridiculous Poopsie much longer, the state police would be sitting in her wagon checking it for fingerprints.

"Please go home," she said as patiently as she could.

But Poopsie stuck out her lower lip. "I'm coming with you," she said. "It's a free country. You can't stop me."

"Oh, yes, I can," Tracy said. "Do you know why? Because I'm not going anywhere now."

Without a backward glance at Poopsie, Tracy marched up her path and into her house.

She knelt on the living room floor and sneaked a look out the window to see if Poopsie was still there.

She was. Her rear stuck up in the air, Poopsie was crawling around on the front lawn, looking at an anthill or something.

Tracy walked into the kitchen to check on Rebel, then settled down by the living room window to wait for Poopsie to give up and go home. Finally Poopsie stood up and skipped down High Flats Road.

"Now," Tracy breathed.

She trotted down the street. When she got near the

empty house, she tried to look as if she weren't paying any attention to it.

No one seemed to be there at all. She continued past the house to make sure, humming and looking unconcerned. But she watched out of the corner of her eye. She walked to the end of the road, and when she still didn't see anyone come out of the house, she decided to take a chance on getting the wagon.

Slowly she walked back to the empty house. Then she raced up the lawn, grabbed the wagon, and ran.

Within a few minutes she was in her own garage, with the wagon. She wiped her perspiring hands on her shirt and sat down until her heart stopped thudding.

Finally she got to her feet. She took the cans of red and green paint out of the wagon and slid them back on the shelf.

Safe!

But was she? Everyone in town would know about the paint on the empty house in a little while. And once they saw the big pink initials on her wagon, it wouldn't take some noseybody long to figure out that Tracy Matson had been the painter.

She'd have to get rid of those initials. She'd just paint them right off. But what color? She didn't want to paint the wagon black; she couldn't paint it green; and she certainly didn't want to paint it red. Perhaps a nice shade of orange would do.

She moved some cans around, but she couldn't find any orange paint. That was the trouble with her father. Much as she loved him, he didn't have much style when it came to color.

At last she settled on a can of gray paint her father

had used to paint the porch floor last summer. She dipped the brush into the gray paint. It made a faint pink smear but she wiggled the paint around with the brush, and in a few minutes the pink had disappeared.

It wasn't easy to cover the initials. She kept going over them until there were about six coats of gray paint on the wagon. The paint looked thick and ugly. But she was so relieved to have the initials erased forever that she didn't care.

Next she cleaned out a corner of the garage by dragging old cardboard cartons full of nails and chains and tools to the center of the floor. Then she pushed the wagon into the corner and put the cartons back in front of it. When she'd finished, the wagon was completely hidden. "Safe now," she said. "No one will ever know."

She closed the garage door behind her and walked toward the house. It was starting to rain. If only it had rained all day, she would have stayed in the house and wouldn't have gotten into the painting project at all.

Why did she always get herself into trouble? she wondered. The more she thought about it, the sadder she became. And those poor old people. They'd have to live in a house they thought a lunatic had painted.

She'd have to make it up to them, and the sooner the better.

But how?

She'd have to earn a pile of money this summer and give it all to them. She'd say that she always donated about one hundred dollars to new neighbors. The people would be able to get their house painted over again, and she'd suggest a nice bright color.

Yes, the old people would probably end up with the

best-looking house on High Flats Road, and they'd owe it all to her.

But she didn't feel comforted at all. And when she thought about all that money, she suddenly realized she'd have to give up the fair. Her heart sank. Wouldn't you know! Leroy and everybody would be having a great time going on all the rides and eating all that terrific food, and where would she be? Home. Counting her pennies.

She started up the back steps and tripped over Poopsie Pomerantz.

"Do you always whisper to yourself like that?" Poopsie asked.

Tracy's mouth opened with shock. "What are you doing here?" she asked.

"Waiting for you." Poopsie sniffled. "I brought a hanky." She waved it in front of Tracy's nose.

"How long have you been here?"

"Just a few minutes," Poopsie said.

Tracy breathed easier. "I have to go in now, Poopsie. Look, it's raining out."

"I know," Poopsie said. "I'm going. I just wanted to ask you—"

"What? Come on. I'm getting soaked."

"How come you painted over the initials on your wagon? It looked nice that way."

Tracy stared at her in horror. Then, without a word, she stepped around her and went into the house to clean her bedroom.

6

The next day was hot. Shimmery waves of heat hovered over High Flats, and locusts shrilled in the trees. In her faded blue bathing suit Tracy headed for the river.

Poopsie was there ahead of her, balancing herself on a red tube that looked like a horse's head, kicking her feet. And Leroy, wet hair plastered to his neck, was jumping off a rock in the deep part of the river.

"Stop that splashing for a minute, will you?" Tracy called to Poopsie. "Let me get myself wet all at once."

Poopsie whinnied a couple of times and moved aside to let Tracy run through the shallows and bellywop into the water.

She surfaced snorting, and with quick strokes swam out to Leroy. "Want to see me dive?" she asked as she pulled herself up on the warm gray rock.

Leroy didn't answer. He jumped up and down on one foot, trying to get some water out of his ear.

"Hold still, Leroy, and listen to me. I can show you a lot of things about diving." She sat on the edge of the rock and dangled her feet in the water. "I may not be so hot about unimportant things like reading, but I know a lot about everything else."

Leroy took two steps, held his nose, and jumped off the rock with a loud splash. When his head popped out of the water, he yelled, "You're not as smart as you think you are, Tracy. Guess what I—" His head disappeared in a froth of bubbles as he swam toward the rock.

She waited for him, heart pounding. Everybody in town was trying to figure out who had painted the empty house. Somehow Leroy must have found out.

He scrambled back up on the rock. "It's about Mrs. Clausson."

"Yes?"

"And her boarders."

"Get on with it, Leroy," Tracy said.

"Have a little patience," Leroy went on. "I'm trying to tell you."

Tracy took a deep breath. She'd really like to sock him right in the mouth. Instead she put on her most patient face and sat there as if she had a million years to wait for him to tell his story.

"My mother told me that Mrs. Clausson has new boarders. They came in late last night. A mother and a father and a girl. Just about our age."

Tracy let out her breath. He didn't know one thing about the house, after all. "How long are they staying?" she asked.

Leroy shrugged. "Who knows?"

She stood up. "Well, I'm going down there right now

and find out all about it." She stood poised at the edge of the rock, then, as Leroy went in feet first, she dove cleanly into the water.

A few minutes later, halfway down the road to Claussons' house, she stopped. "Can't go up there like this," she muttered, "looking like some kind of washed-out blue freak in this old suit and my hair in a big fat glob. I'd better go home first and get myself decent."

She turned back and ran up her path, then raced upstairs to her bedroom.

By tilting the dresser mirror a little and standing on the bed, she could see all of herself from head to toe.

"Yeech," she said.

Her hair was full of knots, her knees were scraped, and pieces of grass from the river's edge were stuck to her muddy legs.

"Yeech," she said again. It was almost too hot to fuss, but she didn't want the new girl to think she was a real mess.

She dashed into the bathroom, turned the water on full force, and dumped some of her mother's best bath oil into the bubbling water.

While she waited for the tub to fill, she rooted around in her dresser drawers and the bottom of her closet for something decent to wear.

What a shame this was Friday. On Saturdays her mother washed her clothes and gave them to her to put away.

Tracy always left everything in a pile somewhere. During the week the pile got mixed up with a lot of other things. By Wednesday or Thursday it was so hard to find any clothes at all that she wore a bathing suit as much as she could.

Tracy dove cleanly into the water.

After her bath she settled on a blue-and-white shorts set that she found, by some miracle, folded over a hanger in the closet.

On the way downstairs she congratulated herself. Her red braids gleamed, and even though the day was stifling, she felt cool and neat.

Looking at her scrubbed face in the hall mirror, she wondered nervously whether anyone would suspect that she was the kind of girl who went around painting other people's houses. She shuddered.

Then slowly and carefully she walked down the middle of High Flats Road, trying not to stir up dust on her clean outfit.

She stopped at Mrs. Clausson's front path. On the porch were about four people—the two old men who had been there before and a couple of ladies. Certainly not a girl her own age. She'd kill that Leroy if she had gotten out of the river for nothing, wasted her whole morning taking a bath, putting on clean clothes and everything.

One of the old men opened his eyes. "Looking for the little girl?" he asked.

So there was a girl.

She nodded and walked up the path, feeling a little nervous. After all, the girl might not be the friendly kind. She could even be a real pest like Mary Grace Hodges in school.

"She's looking for you too, if your name is Tracy," the man said.

"She knows my name?"

"Yup." The man stopped to take a pipe out of his pocket. "I think she's around back in the kitchen with Mrs. Clausson."

Puzzled, Tracy walked around the side of the house to the back and peered through the screen door. "Hey, Mrs. Clausson," she called. "You in there?"

Mrs. Clausson wiped her plump hands on a towel. "Come on in, Tracy."

Tracy stepped into the kitchen, blinking a little to get used to the dim light.

"Bet you've come to help me get lunch ready for the boarders," Mrs. Clausson said. She laughed and wiped some perspiration off her forehead.

"Well, not exactly."

"Maybe some other time."

Tracy nodded. "Right now, though, Mrs. Clausson, I'm looking for someone. Leroy said you have some new boarders."

"Yes, finally got a girl this time. She's in the dining room."

Tracy looked through the doorway. Standing next to the long dining room table was a girl. She had freckles and brown hair that hung in wispy bangs over her forehead. And she was laughing.

"Surprise, Tracy! I'm Casey Valentine, your pen pal. I was just coming to look for you."

7

Tracy stood there, mouth open. "Casey Valentine," she said at last. "What are you doing here?"

Casey grinned at her. "Remember I wrote that I had a surprise for you?" She put her hands on her hips and stuck out her chin. "Ta, da!" she said. "I'm the surprise. My father had some vacation time coming, and Mrs. Moles, our next-door neighbor—" She broke off. "Remember Walter Moles, your old pen pal, who was here last summer?"

Tracy nodded.

"Well, his mother talked my mother and father into coming here."

"Casey Valentine." Tracy shook her head. "I can't believe it. Hey. Where's your sister, Van?"

"She didn't want to leave her friends so she's staying with Sue Verona."

Behind them Mrs. Clausson closed the oven door.

"Why don't you two get out of this hot house? Go up to the river or play a game somewhere?"

"How about the river?" Tracy asked as they started up High Flats Road. "Can you row?"

Casey hesitated. "Not really."

"I'll teach you in nothing flat. I'm good at that. Come on," she said, cutting across Mrs. Grant's front lawn to get to her driveway faster. "We'll stop at my house first. Get some potato salad from last night's supper and spread it on a roll or something. Then we won't waste twenty years worrying about coming back for lunch."

She banged open the back door and stepped over Rebel, who was dozing in the middle of the kitchen floor. "My dog," she said, waving her hand at him. "A little on the fat side. Eats too much." She reached into the cabinet and threw him a dog biscuit.

Without getting up, Rebel lolled out his wide pink tongue to scoop up the biscuit. Casey sank down beside him on the floor and stroked his bristly back. "Wow," she said. "This is the fattest dog I've ever seen."

Tracy shrugged. "I'm going to put him on a diet soon. Maybe tomorrow." She slid the bowl of potato salad out of the refrigerator onto the table and ran her finger around the edge of the bowl.

On the counter the phone began to ring. "Probably my mother," Tracy said, licking the mayonnaise off her finger. "Calls from work every once in a while to check up on me. Wants to make sure I'm still alive."

She reached for the receiver. "Hello, Mom?" She cradled it between her ear and her shoulder and began to spread potato salad on rolls from the breadbox.

"Reading?" she said into the phone. She held it tighter to her ear to make sure Casey couldn't hear what her mother was saying on the other end. "Mmm, yes," she said. "Going to get to it as soon as possible."

She listened for a minute, then clicked her teeth silently with her tongue. "This afternoon? Well"—she paused and glanced at Casey—"my pen pal is here. Casey Valentine. Staying at Mrs. Clausson's for a while. I'm going to show her how to row."

She sighed. "All right. I'll get to it before supper. 'Bye."

Her back toward Casey, she put the receiver on the hook. That whole reading business was some nuisance, a complete waste of time.

"Did I hear you say something about reading to your mother?" Casey asked.

Tracy shoved the sandwiches into a brown paper bag. "I guess so."

"I love to read," Casey said. "I'm going to be a mystery writer when I grow up. Do you have a library here?"

"In the next town. Windsor. We'd have to go by bike."

"What have you read this summer?"

"Let's see." Tracy pretended to think. "I can't remember."

Casey looked at her curiously. "You don't remember?"

"I read so much," Tracy began, mumbling, then broke off. "That reminds me," she said quickly. "I hope you'll be here for the County Fair. We'll have such a good time. They have about a million rides and ten million things to eat. There's corn on the cob dripping

with butter and salt, and purple cotton candy, and
caramel apples, and soft ice cream—"

"Stop," yelled Casey, tossing her bangs out of her
eyes. "I'm starving."

"The trouble is we need money. Lots of money. But
don't worry. We have two weeks to earn it. We should
have hundreds by that time."

"At least." Casey grinned. "Maybe thousands."

"I'm glad you didn't ask me how we're going to earn
it. That's what we have to figure out."

"I'm good at that," Casey said. "Any time you need
an idea . . ."

"Well, it better be a new idea," Tracy said. "Everyone in High Flats will be trying to earn money. And in
Windsor too. You'll be falling over people who want to
mow your lawn and kids with lemonade stands." She
paused, thinking about the house she had painted and
the money she needed for that.

"Maybe we could do a newspaper. Remember, I did
one in school last year," Casey said.

"Well," Tracy replied slowly, "I don't know how
much money we could earn that way. There aren't that
many kids around here."

"I'll keep thinking."

Tracy nodded. "Good. We have a couple of days
before we have to decide. Right now let's get down to
the river before this whole afternoon is over."

They sped up High Flats Road to the river and slid
over the rocks to the Matsons' rowboat. Tracy untied it
and pushed off into the current.

When they reached the center of the river, she said,
"Watch me, then you can try." She dipped the oars
smoothly into the water.

"Watch me, then you can try," Tracy said.

For a few minutes Casey watched her. "I think I've got it now," she said.

Tracy nodded. "All right, then. We'll switch seats. Don't worry. The water isn't deep. Not over your head anyway."

Carefully they changed places. Casey sat in the middle of the boat. She grabbed the oars and sloshed them into the water.

They left a trail of bubbles as they went slowly down the river, swerving from one side to the other. The oars grated loudly against the oarlocks.

Tracy could hardly stand it.

Out of the corner of her eye she could see Leroy and Richard on the bridge. She certainly hoped they didn't think she was doing that horrible rowing.

"You could straighten out a little," she suggested.

"I know. I'm trying the best I can. It just seems to come out crooked," Casey panted. Beads of perspiration had popped out on her forehead. She ran her tongue over her braces, then let go of one oar and wiped her face, leaving a long gray smudge on her cheek.

"Watch out for the oar," Tracy yelled. But it was too late. Casey grabbed for it, but the oar popped out of the oarlock, slid into the water, and gently drifted away.

Casey looked at Tracy. "Yikes," she said. "Now what?"

"Nothing to it," Tracy replied. She slipped over the side of the boat and splashed into the water.

"Feels good," she said. In less than a minute she grabbed the oar, and still watching Leroy and Richard,

who were looking at the boat with interest, she hauled herself back in.

"Are they laughing at us?" Casey asked, noticing the boys on the bridge for the first time.

Tracy glared up at them. "Pair of idiots," she said. "Don't pay any attention to them. Just makes them act up more."

"Probably like Gunther Reed at home," Casey said. "Sometimes he can be a pest too."

By this time they were approaching the bridge. Tracy glanced up at its open grillwork. "They like to drop things through on top of the boats."

"Like what?"

"Fish heads, fish guts, sometimes smashed tomatoes —anything they have handy, especially if it's wet and gooky."

Casey shuddered.

"That's Leroy and Richard up there. Sometimes we're friends, but most of the time we're enemies. Now there are two of us, though. They won't be able to get away with a thing."

Suddenly it was shady as they moved under the bridge. Tracy looked up as she heard the boys pounding back and forth over her head, giggling. "Speed it up, Casey. They're up to something." She clicked her teeth. "Should have rowed past the bridge myself."

Tongue hanging out with concentration, Casey started to row faster.

"Watch where you're going," Tracy shouted.

But it was too late. With a jarring bump, the boat hit the rocks on the side of the bridge.

"*Sacrebleu*," Casey exclaimed.

Above them, Leroy lay flat on the bridge and pushed

a night crawler through the open grillwork. The worm landed on top of Tracy's head, slid onto her lap, and down her leg to the bottom of the rowboat. A moment later, a sucker came hurtling through the air and flapped on the seat next to Casey.

"Don't be afraid of it," Tracy told her. "Just toss it over the side."

"I'm not afraid," Casey answered. "I did an experiment with some dead fish last year." She picked up the sucker gingerly with two fingers and put it over the side. "What a pair of weasels," she said as Tracy stood up, grabbed an oar, and poled it against the rocks to push the boat into deeper water. The boys cackled above as the girls drifted away from the bridge along the shoreline.

"Let's rest awhile," Tracy said. She nosed the boat into a marshy indentation and stuck her legs over the side. The mud at the water's edge cooled her bare feet. A frog, no larger than her pinky fingernail, hopped across her instep and disappeared into the weeds that lined the shore.

Casey leaned over the side of the boat. "I didn't know that frogs came so small," she said.

"There's a hair snake," Tracy said, pointing. The snake, as fine as a strand of blond hair, wiggled its way around in a shallow puddle. She broke off a twig from one of the bushes and tried to make the snake wind itself around it.

Suddenly she sat up straight.

"Casey, I just thought of a way to get back at old Leroy."

"*Très bien*," Casey said. "That means terrific, I think."

"Do you know the French word for hair snake?" Tracy said.

"Of course not. I only know about twenty-five words, and I've been trying to learn French from Walter's grandmother."

"Well, everyone in High Flats knows that hair snakes live at the edge of the river in the mud. Everyone, that is, except—maybe Leroy. After all, he just moved here from Binghamton last winter."

She leaned over the side of the boat, scooped up the snake on a wet leaf, and put it carefully under her seat. "Leroy is finished, Casey. Just stick with me and by tomorrow he'll be ashamed to walk down High Flats Road in the daytime."

"How—" Casey began and stopped. "What was that noise?"

Both girls were silent, listening. Droplets of water trickled off the ends of the oars and plinked into the water.

"Yipes. It's the four o'clock whistle from the factory in Windsor. My mother will be home soon." She pulled up the anchor.

Bending over the oars, she rowed up the river and scrambled out of the boat ahead of Casey to loop the wet boat rope over the iron post. Then she bent over and picked up the hair snake.

"Come on," she yelled. "I have to get a jar for this snake, and make my bed, and let the water out of the tub, and—" She shut her mouth quickly. She still had to read for fifteen minutes before supper, but Casey didn't have to know that.

8

After supper Tracy and Casey hunted around until they spotted Leroy across the street from Mrs. Clausson's. He was in the backyard, helping Mr. Jensen fix his lawn mower. Leaning first on one foot and then on the other, the girls waited at the side of the garage while Mr. Jensen fiddled with the motor. Finally he said to Leroy, "I guess that'll do it now. Looks as if we fixed her as good as new."

As Leroy walked around the garage on his way home, Tracy stepped out of the shadows. She cleared her throat. "Catch any fish today?"

Leroy jumped back in surprise. "Why are you hiding back here?"

"Scared you, didn't we? You're not too brave, I see," Tracy answered. "This is my pen pal, Casey Valentine, and, as a matter of fact, we're waiting for you."

Leroy nodded at Casey. "I wasn't afraid," he grumbled. "But I didn't expect you to be lurking around in the dark. What do you want anyway?"

"I thought I'd do you a little favor," she said. "If you take our advice, you'll probably be rich by the end of the summer."

"What are you talking about?" Leroy asked.

"Hair snakes," Tracy said.

"Richard is right. Something is loose in your head." He started down the path.

Casey swished air through her braces. "You lost your big chance, Leroy," she said. "At least a hundred dollars just went down the drain."

Reluctantly he turned back to them. "Are you serious?"

"Are you the only kid in town with blond hair?" Tracy asked.

"I guess so," said Leroy, considering. "Right."

"For some reason, only people with yellow hair can make hair snakes," said Tracy.

"And of course you know how valuable they are," Casey added.

Leroy nodded uncertainly.

Tracy moved a little closer to him. "All you have to do, Leroy, is put a piece of your hair in a jar of river water. Tonight. Leave it on the porch in the air. By tomorrow it will be a hair snake—alive—ready for sale."

"And you'll be on the way to a pile of money," Casey said.

"A piece of hair can't become alive," he said. "Can it?"

"It's alive on your head, isn't it? I guess the river

"Can you keep a secret?" Tracy asked.

water revives it. Must be proteins or chemicals or something," Casey said.

"Can you keep a secret?" Tracy asked. "I wouldn't want this to get around."

"Sure, Tracy. Sure I can," he answered.

"Do you remember Paul Stewart?" Tracy asked. "The kid who lived in Jensens' house before they bought it?"

Leroy shook his head. "I didn't live here then."

"Well," Tracy said, "Paul moved away after he had sold about a million hair snakes at fifty cents each."

"Mrs. Clausson told me about him," Casey went on. "He bought a mansion in some rich neighborhood. It has thirty rooms. Can you imagine? He's eleven years old and already he's retired. He doesn't even bother to go to school."

"Why should he?" Tracy broke in. "He doesn't have to get anywhere in life. He's there already." She bit at a ragged edge of fingernail. "Of course, Paul overdid it a little."

"Yes," said Casey. "He's as bald as an egg now."

For a few seconds Leroy stood there, his mouth open. Then he snapped it shut. "I'll do it," he said. "Sure I will."

As Leroy scampered down the driveway, Tracy turned back to Casey, who was biting her lip to keep from laughing. "No smarter than the suckers in the river," Tracy said, looking after him. "Just one big dummy."

They stayed there in the dark until they thought Leroy had had enough time to get home, find a jar, and put one of his blond hairs in it. Then, sure that

by this time he must be in bed, they started across the street for Tracy's house to get the hair snake.

"Casey," a voice called from Mrs. Clausson's front porch. "Time to come in."

The girls stopped and looked at each other. "My mother," Casey said.

"Casey," Mrs. Valentine called again.

"Five minutes more?" Casey begged.

"Now," said her mother. "It's pitch-black out. Time for bed."

"Never mind," Tracy said. "I'll put the snake in Leroy's bottle. You'll be around in the morning to see what's happened."

Tracy stood watching Casey trudge down High Flats Road to Mrs. Clausson's, then she tiptoed up her own driveway. If her mother heard her, she'd probably have to go in too.

She went into the garage, picked up the bottle with the snake in it, and crossed the road to Leroy's house. Light from the living room windows lay in patches on the painted gray planks of the porch floor. Inside, Mrs. Wilson was playing the piano. It was the kind of music Tracy liked, loud with lots of heavy, crashing notes.

She tiptoed up the steps and onto the porch. She ducked as she passed the living room window. She could see Mrs. Wilson at the piano and Mr. Wilson reading the paper.

She searched around, looking for Leroy's jar. Spotting it on the edge of the railing, she shook her head. Just about what you'd expect, she thought. The first wind that came along would knock that jar right off the porch.

She could imagine how it would be tomorrow. Leroy would parade up and down the street with the hair snake in the bottle. He'd try to sell the snake to some little kid like Poopsie for a dollar, and she'd tell him he was crazy. The whole round world would be laughing.

Tracy almost felt sorry for him. Yes, she did feel sorry for him. Even though he didn't deserve it. Maybe she'd just get out of there and skip the whole thing.

The porch floor creaked as she took a step. She stopped, absolutely still, one foot in the air.

The piano stopped too. For a moment Tracy thought someone had heard her, but Mrs. Wilson's voice drifted faintly through the window. She was talking with Mr. Wilson.

Tracy put her foot down and tilted her head curiously, trying to hear what they were saying. But hard as she tried, she could hear only bits of the conversation with a lot of buzzing in between.

"That foolish boy, Leroy," Mrs. Wilson said. "Buzz, buzz—what he's up to now."

Mr. Wilson rattled the paper and grunted.

"Says he'll be rich by tomorrow. Buzz, buzz—going to buy me a diamond ring."

Tracy swiveled around so she could see in the window.

Mr. Wilson was buried behind the paper, and Mrs. Wilson had moved away from the piano. She sat on the couch flipping through a magazine. "Wouldn't tell me," Mrs. Wilson went on, "but you can bet—buzz, buzz—Tracy's middle name should be trouble."

Too bad for you, Leroy, Tracy thought. She held up his bottle. Inside were two long blond hairs in a little

water. He's not taking any chances, she thought, with just one hair. She fished them out. Then she took the hair snake out of her bottle and dropped it into his.

Turning, she glanced back into the living room window. Mr. Wilson had lowered his paper. "If I had a daughter like Tracy, I'd have gray hair," he said clearly. "She gets herself into all kinds of messes because she doesn't do what she's supposed to."

"And then," Mrs. Wilson added, "she acts like a know-it-all. Thinks people won't notice. Buzz, buzz— never thinks about anyone else's feelings."

Tracy took a step backward. She felt a knot of anger in her chest. "Liars," she said. "Mean."

She took another step backward. Her elbow grazed the jar on the railing. It tipped over and fell on the floor, spilling the water as it rolled along the porch. The snake slithered away through the porch railing and disappeared into the bushes.

By this time, Mr. and Mrs. Wilson were at the front door.

Without looking backward, Tracy vaulted the porch railing and tore across High Flats Road for home.

"What's going on out here?" Mr. Wilson yelled. "Tracy is that you?"

Out of breath, she leaned against the side of her house and looked back toward the Wilsons' front porch. Mr. Wilson had gone inside, but Mrs. Wilson stood there looking out at High Flats Road. Tracy ducked back into the shadows and watched until Mrs. Wilson finally went in and closed the door behind her.

Slowly Tracy walked around to the back of her house. It was so dark she could hardly see the steps. She put her foot on the first one as quietly as she could.

All she needed now was her mother popping out the back door wanting to know what was going on. She put her foot on the next step and sprawled over her tackle box, spilling hooks, bobbles, and lures down the steps.

"Brown scabby knees for the rest of the summer," she moaned, holding her skinned knee.

The porch light clicked on from inside the house. "Are you all right, Tracy?" her mother asked. "What's going on out there? I thought you were upstairs."

"I'm not," she answered. "I mean I'm all right. I'm not upstairs."

Her mother poked her head out the door. "What was that crash?"

"Knocked over my tackle box. Leave the light on, please, so I can pick everything up."

"It's late, Tracy. Time for bed."

"I'll be right in."

"Hurry up," her mother said and closed the door.

Tracy ran her hand gingerly along the steps. "Watch out," she muttered to herself. "Don't want a fish hook in my finger."

"Talking to yourself?" a voice asked behind her.

Tracy jumped. On the lawn stood Poopsie Pomerantz. She had on pink flannel pajamas. Over them she wore her mother's brown wool sweater with the sleeves rolled up in clumps around her elbows.

"What are you doing out so late?" Tracy asked.

Poopsie sat on the bottom step. "Couldn't sleep. My mother said I could sit outside for a minute. My allergies are bad tonight. See?" She sniffled as loud as she could and ran the sweater sleeve across her nose. "Can't breathe."

Tracy shuddered. "Stop that, you're disgusting."

Poopsie nodded cheerfully. "Everybody says that."

"Besides," Tracy continued, "why are you wearing all those clothes? Aren't you ready to suffocate from the heat?"

"My grandmother is staying with us this week. She says I should watch out for the night air, or I'll catch cold."

"How would you even know the difference?" Tracy asked. "You're always sneezing and sniffling anyway."

"What went on at the Wilsons'?" Poopsie asked.

"Nothing much." Tracy groped around, looking for the missing lures.

"Nothing much? Lights going on, people yelling—"

"Just a little misunderstanding."

"What little misunderstanding?"

"Mrs. Wilson—" Tracy started and paused. "It's really too long to go into. By the time I explain everything it'll be midnight."

Poopsie sniffed. "I heard Mrs. Wilson say that there's no peace in this whole town because of you."

Tracy clicked her teeth. "She thinks she's the boss of the world."

"She's pretty nice to me. The other day—"

"Stop sniffling like that," Tracy interrupted. "Blow your nose, will you?"

Poopsie reached up under the sweater sleeve and pulled out a wad of toilet paper. "Ran out of hankies," she said apologetically.

"The trouble with Mrs. Wilson," Tracy said, ignoring the toilet paper, "is that she's still mad at me because I needed some of her flowers for school. For my teacher." A lot of good those flowers did, she

thought. Mrs. Graham had still given her a terrible report card.

"Mrs. Wilson told my mother you took all her roses."

"Mrs. Wilson has about a thousand roses. I just cut a few. She made such a fuss you'd think I'd cut off her arm instead of a few miserable flowers."

Poopsie stuffed the toilet paper back in her sweater sleeve. "I started to tell you, Tracy. Mrs. Wilson asked me to tell her my name."

"Pretty silly question, if you ask me."

"I mean my real name."

Tracy looked at her curiously. "Why?"

"I guess my mother told her I hate being called Poopsie."

"What's your real name anyway?"

"Celeste."

Tracy snickered. "You don't look like a Celeste to me."

"Well, Mrs. Wilson said she's going to call me Celeste from now on."

Tracy picked up the last lure and dropped it into her tackle box. "I'm sick of the whole Wilson family." She stood up. "You'd better get along home, Poopsie, and forget the whole Celeste idea for a couple of years. I'm going inside now."

Tracy opened the kitchen door and waited until Poopsie was out of sight. Then she snapped off the porch light and went upstairs to bed.

9

Tracy was half asleep the next morning when her mother opened her bedroom door. In her arms was a pile of Tracy's clothes.

"I'm on my way to work, Tracy," she said, "but I thought I'd run up here with some clean clothes first." She slid the clothes out of her arms onto the dresser. A pair of socks, rolled into a ball, slipped off the top of the pile and disappeared under the bed.

Her mother knelt down and reached under the bed for them.

"Tracy Matson," she said, her face red, as she stood up again, "I can't believe that mess under your bed. I'm really ashamed of you."

Tracy sat up. "I know. It's a little sloppy."

"A little! Tracy, when are you going to learn to do something because it's the right thing to do and not because someone is yelling at you?"

"Today," Tracy said.

"I hope so," her mother said, looking at her watch. "I really do." She bent over and kissed Tracy. "I'm late for work. I have to go." She looked at Tracy for a minute longer. "Think about what I said." Then she walked out of the room and hurried down the stairs.

Five minutes later Tracy heard Casey call for her. She knelt on the bed and flattened her nose against the window screen. "Up here," she called.

"The worst rower in the world is here to get you out of bed," Casey yelled back.

"Be right down." Tracy grabbed an orange polo shirt and shrugged it over her head. Who cared that the shirt didn't match her red plaid shorts or that the shorts had a small rip from a fish hook? Casey was her friend now. She wasn't going to waste her time putting on special clothes every two minutes.

She started down the stairs, then remembered the mess under her bed. Turning back, she yelled out the hall window to Casey. "Sit on the steps a second, will you? I'll be there as fast as I can."

She got down on her hands and knees next to the bed and pulled out a banana peel, two bowls, and a bunch of games. There was a library book, too. Let it stay under there, she thought. As fast as she could, she piled the games on top of each other and took them over to the closet. It was a good thing, she thought, that her closet was big and very dark. She slung the games in the back, ignoring the sound of the marbles that rolled out of the box onto the floor.

Then she went back to the bed, looped the banana peel over the bowls, and raced downstairs with them.

On her way past the front door to the kitchen, she held
the door open with one hand. "Come on in," she told
Casey. "I have to have a decent breakfast today."

Casey followed her into the kitchen.

"My mother found out," she continued, "that I've
been having two orange ice pops every morning."

Casey laughed. "How did she find that out?"

"There weren't any left in the freezer, and she
wanted to know why. When I told her, she said we
can't buy any pops until I finish this box of Crispies
cereal."

Tracy peered into the box and frowned. "It's probably about five days' worth." She poured some cereal
and milk into Rebel's bowl and took some for herself.

Rebel stood up, stretched, and padded over to his
bowl. He sniffed at the cereal, then went back under
the kitchen table to finish his nap.

"Ignorant dog," Tracy said. "Doesn't want a decent
breakfast. Likes orange ice pops better." She sat down
at the table and began eating.

"Don't you have any orange juice or toast?" Casey
asked.

"My mother did mention something about juice, I
think." Tracy reached over to open the refrigerator and
looked at a bottle of root beer. Shrugging, she pulled
out the orange juice and set it on the table. "Want
some?"

"I just finished breakfast."

Tracy picked up her spoon and dug into the cereal.

"Hey, you haven't told me yet about last night,"
Casey said. "Did you put the hair snake in Leroy's
bottle?"

Tracy stopped eating, spoon halfway to her mouth. "Hair snake," she said. She stared at Casey, trying to think of something to say, but all she could think of was Mr. Wilson saying that she didn't do what she was supposed to do. She'd just like to forget that whole hair snake business. "The snake just wiggled away somehow," she said at last, making waving motions in the air with the spoon. Crispies and milk dripped on the table. "Gone forever."

Casey swished her braces. "Can't we get another one?"

"Sometimes they're hard to get," she answered. She dug into the cereal again.

"Come on, Tracy," Casey said. "There must be another reason."

"Got caught," Tracy answered slowly. "Jar rolled off the porch and the Wilsons came running out. They probably thought I was a robber." She giggled half-heartedly. "I escaped, though. They're not really sure it was me."

Casey nodded. "Don't worry," she said. "We'll think of something else. I told you I'm good at ideas."

"Right," Tracy said. "Well, what's it going to be today? A little fishing?" She put some Crispies in her mouth and chewed.

"How about the library?" Casey suggested. "We could get a couple of books and read in the boat."

Tracy nearly choked on the Crispies. That would ruin a perfectly good day. Thinking fast, she swallowed and shook her head. "You'd need a bike."

Casey beamed at her. "Mrs. Clausson said she has an old one in the cellar she'll lend me."

Tracy frowned. She ate some more Crispies. She wasn't going to spend the afternoon reading in a rowboat. Not this afternoon, not any afternoon. She could imagine what Leroy and Richard would say if they saw her.

"Someone calling you?" Casey asked.

Tracy heard a sniffle outside. She lifted her cereal bowl to her mouth, draining the last of the sugary milk, and went to the window. "You want something, Poopsie?" She wiped away a milk mustache.

"Can I come in?"

"I'm a little busy now. Come back later." She went back to the kitchen table.

"I suppose we're going to have her hanging around all day," Tracy told Casey.

"Who is she?"

"Lives down the road. Nice little kid, I suppose, if you can get past her nose."

"You mean it's big?"

"No. Wet. She's allergic to the whole world."

"I am not."

Tracy jumped. Poopsie stood at the back door, nose pressed against the screen.

"I am not," Poopsie repeated.

"Not what?" Tracy asked.

"Allergic to the whole world. I'm just allergic to hay and grass and chocolate. Stuff like that."

Tracy shrugged and turned to Casey. "Did you notice how hard it is to get a little privacy in this town?"

"I see you're eating Crispies," Poopsie said. "It's my favorite kind."

"Let her in," Casey said.

"Be my guest, Poopsie," Tracy muttered.

Poopsie opened the back door slowly and came into the kitchen. "I heard about you," she said to Casey. "You're Tracy's pen pal."

Casey smiled. "Hi, Poopsie. That's right."

Poopsie turned to Tracy. "Don't worry," she said. "I brought my hanky this time."

"Make sure you use it," Tracy said, frowning.

"I'll fix the cereal myself," Poopsie offered as Tracy continued to sit at the kitchen table.

Tracy waved her hand toward the refrigerator. "Go ahead."

Poopsie reached in for a bottle of milk. "What are you kids going to do today anyway?"

"We were trying to decide that when we were interrupted," Tracy said.

"You should show the new girl the empty house," Poopsie said. "Somebody sure messed it up. Gobs of paint all over the place. Everybody in town is wondering what kind of sick-o would—"

"I guess we're going to the library now," Tracy broke in quickly.

Poopsie opened her eyes wide. "You're going to the library? That's a hot one. What for?"

Tracy could have screamed. "To get a book, numbskull." She turned to Casey. "I have to get my library book out of my bedroom. I'll be right back."

She raced upstairs as fast as she could. She hated to leave Poopsie alone with Casey any longer than she had to. Who knew what horrible things Poopsie could think of to tell her next!

She looked under her bed and dragged out the book, looking at it curiously. She had read only the first seven pages and by now had forgotten what the whole thing was about.

She tucked it under her arm and went back down to the kitchen.

Poopsie looked up. "I was just telling Casey about the fair. I have two dollars already that I saved from my birthday."

"We've got to get cracking on that," Tracy said, suddenly remembering that she needed a lot more money than usual. She shook herself. "Hurry up with your cereal," she told Poopsie irritably, "so we can get out of here."

"Don't worry about me," Poopsie replied. "I'll just sit here and finish up my Crispies. I can't come anyway. My bike's broken."

"I don't remember inviting you," Tracy said. "Come on, Casey, let's go." She pointed to the garage. "Have to get my bike." Over her shoulder she said to Poopsie, "Wash out your bowl and don't forget to close the back door."

A few minutes later Tracy straddled her bike. "Kid's unbelievable, isn't she?"

"I feel a little sorry for her," Casey answered.

"Don't worry about Poopsie." Tracy patted the handlebars. "Hop on, we'll get your bike."

At Mrs. Clausson's house they wiped the cobwebs off the old bike she had found for Casey. It wasn't long before they were on High Flats Road, heading toward Hubbell Mountain.

Casey shrieked. "Tracy, look at that house!" She braked to a stop.

Tracy pedaled faster. "Come on," she said. "It's just a house. Some lunatic painted it up a little bit."

"A little!" Casey shouted. "What a mess." She got back on the bike and caught up with Tracy, who had reached the road over the mountain.

Tracy felt her face burning. She was glad they had to pedal too hard on the winding road to talk.

Twenty minutes later they sailed down the hill to Windsor. Outside the library Tracy slammed her bike into the rack, motioned to Casey to follow her, and tiptoed in.

Inside it was cool and dark and very quiet. Miss Prince was sitting at her desk.

"Good afternoon, Tracy," she said. "I think your book is overdue again."

"I guess so. I've been a little busy. I've brought a friend, Casey Valentine. She's staying at Mrs. Clausson's for a while. Can she take out books?"

Miss Prince looked at Casey. Finally she nodded. "I'll give you a temporary card, Casey. You look like a girl who washes her hands before she reads." Miss Prince frowned at Tracy. "I wish you'd wash your hands once in a while, Tracy. The books always look so grimy when you finish them."

"I think we'll look for our books now," Tracy said and wandered over to the book stacks ahead of Casey.

"Psst," Casey whispered a few minutes later. "Here's one."

Tracy looked at the letters and sounded them out to herself: *Early Monkeys*. What a peculiar thing for Casey to be interested in!

Casey beamed at her. "Just what we need for the fair."

She was glad she had to pedal too hard to talk.

Tracy grinned weakly. "Sure. If this is what you want to read about, let's take it."

She certainly didn't want to hurt Casey's feelings. "Didn't you say you wanted to be a writer when you grew up?"

"Yes. Mystery stories. Stuff like that. Why?"

"I thought you changed your mind, that maybe you wanted to be a veterinarian or work in a zoo."

"*Sacrebleu.* What made you think that?" Casey asked, wrinkling her forehead.

"I don't know." Tracy tucked the book under her arm and quickly looked at another shelf.

"Let's go look in the L's," Casey said, moving to another stack.

Tracy leaned over Casey's shoulder and saw a bright yellow book with a picture of a girl on the cover. The girl had braids like Tracy's. She looked as if she'd hate to sit around and waste time reading. Tracy knew it was a girl she'd like. Maybe she'd give it a try.

Casey looked at her approvingly. "If you've never read Pippi, you'll love her."

Tracy left Casey kneeling in front of the L's and went to the librarian's desk to check out her books.

"Have you caught a glimpse of your new principal yet?" Miss Prince asked.

"I didn't even know we were getting one." Tracy grinned. Anything new at school had to be an improvement.

"I understand she's going to be a neighbor of yours."

For a moment Tracy stared at the librarian, trying to make sense of what she was saying. A new principal? In High Flats? Nobody had moved to High Flats

except for the people whose house Tracy had painted.
Could it be? Thunderation!

Tracy cleared her throat. "Does she have a white
streak in her hair?"

"I haven't met her yet. Mrs. Clausson stopped in for
some books yesterday and told me about her. Her
name is Mrs. Bemus."

"I haven't seen anybody much around there for the
last few weeks. But I did see a man and woman a week
or so ago," Tracy said slowly.

"That's right. Mrs. Clausson said they've been back
and forth between here and the city."

Tracy's mouth felt dry. She hadn't painted just any
old house. She had actually painted the new principal's house.

At the very least she'd be expelled.

She could hardly swallow. She tried to say good-bye
to Miss Prince, but the words wouldn't come. Instead
she nodded politely, grabbed up her two books, and
went outside to wait for Casey.

10

At Mrs. Clausson's Tracy waved good-bye to Casey and continued up High Flats Road. She pedaled around to her yard and leaned her bike against the back porch.

Now she understood why Mrs. Bemus hadn't done anything about the house. No questions . . . no police . . . no anything. Probably the new principal was waiting until school started and she got to know the children. Then—*bam!*—she'd figure it out. And Tracy would be in for it!

For a few minutes she stood there tracing a pattern in the dusty soil with her sneaker. There was no sense in waiting for Mrs. Bemus to discover who she was. It was time to march herself up there and confess.

Squaring her shoulders, she headed down the path to High Flats Road. Now that she had made up her

mind to tell the truth, she felt a little better. She pretended to be a soldier entering enemy territory. Marching to the middle of the road, she called out in her most military voice, "Hup, two, three, four, hup—" and interrupted herself when she spotted Leroy swishing his old golf club through the grass in front of his house.

She hoped he hadn't heard her. To cover her embarrassment, she said, "You should stay out of that tall grass. It's rattlesnake weather. They come down out of the mountains this time of the year to get water."

"That's probably a big story just like the hair snake." He moved quickly out of the grass onto the paved road. "I'll get you for that, Tracy. Just you wait."

"That was just a joke about the hair snake," she said. "But it's true about the rattlers. Too bad you haven't lived here long. Experts can always tell when rattlers are around. They smell like cucumbers."

Leroy glared at her. "You're crazy," he said. "Loony. My mother said—"

Tracy shrugged and started down High Flats Road again. Actually she had told him the truth . . . mostly. Rattlers were supposed to smell like cucumbers. But there hadn't been a rattler in High Flats for about fifty years. She smiled to herself.

Behind her, Leroy yelled, "Hup, hup, two, three, four, hup."

"Oh, shut up, Leroy," she called over her shoulder.

"Hup, hup, hup," he shouted.

Tracy bent down and picked up a small stone. Turning, she flung it toward Leroy's bike, which was lying next to a tree. She missed. But she hit Leroy on the shin.

He hopped around on the pavement while Tracy watched him.

"Just wait, Tracy. Just you wait till your father comes home. I'm going to be there right in front of your house waiting for him. You know what he said the last time you threw something at me? I'm going to tell him that you're throwing rocks again."

"Rocks!" she shouted, outraged.

"Yeah, rocks."

"That was a little pebble, and you know it, Leroy." Tracy narrowed her eyes. "If you tell my father anything, you'll regret it. Believe me, Leroy, you'll be one sorry kid."

She scurried down the road before Leroy had a chance to answer. "Everything in the whole round world has to go wrong at once," she muttered. "Neighbors turning out to be principals and Leroy always turning up to cause trouble."

By this time she was in front of the Bemus house. She shuddered as she looked at it. She noticed that there was a car in the driveway. "The old Tracy luck," she moaned. "Wouldn't you know someone would have to be home!"

After she rang the bell, she waited a long time. When no one came, she leaned her ear against the door and listened, but everything seemed quiet inside. Then she stood on tiptoe and peered in the little window in the door, but she couldn't see anything.

Finally she turned and started back down the steps.

The door burst open. Mrs. Bemus stood there in a pair of jeans and a yellow halter top. "Sorry it took me

so long," she said, smiling at Tracy. "I was in the bathroom."

Tracy looked up at her, surprised. She knew, of course, that principals went to the bathroom just like everybody else. But it was still hard to believe. And she certainly had never seen a principal in jeans before. This lady seemed very different from the principals Tracy knew. Maybe there'd be a lot of different things happening next year.

Tracy was so interested in the idea that she almost forgot why she was there. Mrs. Bemus looked at her expectantly. Finally she smiled back at Mrs. Bemus. "I'm Tracy Matson," she said. "I'm in your school and I live down the street."

"Hello, Tracy Matson," Mrs. Bemus said. She sat on the front steps. With a pat of her hand, she invited Tracy to sit down too.

"Do you have any pets?" Mrs. Bemus asked.

"A dog," Tracy answered. "A fat dog. His name is Rebel."

"Great. How would you like to do something for an old lady?"

"Sure. Are you the old lady?"

Mrs. Bemus laughed. "How tactful you are!"

Tracy laughed too. "I didn't mean—"

"It's all right." She waved her hand. "What I really need is food for my cat. If you'd lend me a can of dog food, maybe I could mash it for her. I've just come from the city, and all I have in the refrigerator is a bottle of orange juice, a bag of wilted celery, and two tomatoes. I don't have the energy to take the car two miles to the store."

"That's easy," Tracy said. "And you don't have to worry about dog food. I'll catch a little fish for your cat." She wrinkled her forehead. "A bass, I think. Pickerel is too bony."

"Could you really?" Mrs. Bemus looked impressed.

"Sure. I'll leave it on your back porch." Tracy jumped off the steps and started down the path.

"Hey," Mrs. Bemus called after her. "I like you, Tracy Matson."

Tracy grinned and raced down to Mrs. Clausson's to call for Casey. An hour later they left a small silver bass, neatly cleaned and boned on Mrs. Bemus's porch.

It wasn't until she was finishing supper that night that she remembered why she had gone to Mrs. Bemus's house in the first place. She started to get up.

"Where are you going, young lady?" her father asked. "You haven't finished your rhubarb yet."

Tracy sat down again. It was better to eat the slimy rhubarb, she thought, than to go to Mrs. Bemus's house and tell her the truth.

"Another thing," her father said, "I haven't noticed that you're doing much reading this summer. Are you getting in your fifteen minutes a day?"

Tracy was silent for a moment. She really couldn't tell him that she was saving up the time and marking down on a piece of paper how many minutes she owed. Then she spotted her father's newspaper on the counter. "I could read to you a little bit right now," she said. "Right out of your newspaper."

Her father nodded. "Good idea."

Tracy reached for the paper and began to read while her father drank his coffee. "Suffer thunderstorms hunt creeps in the wet," she said in a slow, loud voice.

Her father put his cup down. "Good grief, Tracy, let me see that." He shook his head. "You mean, 'Severe Thunderstorms Hurt Crops in the West.'" He tossed the paper back on the counter. "You'd better get yourself upstairs to your room after the dishes and read from your own book. And from now on, make it twenty minutes."

11

"Shrubbery," Casey said.

Tracy scratched the scab on her knee. "Caterpillar."

"That sounds good. How about tapioca pudding?"

"No good. That's two words."

Mrs. Matson stuck her head out of the kitchen door. It was Saturday and she was home, writing checks to pay bills. "What are you two doing?" she asked.

"We're saying words that sound nice in our mouths," Tracy answered.

"You mean words like roller coaster?" Mrs. Matson asked.

"Right." Tracy smiled at her. "Except that roller coaster is two words and we're doing one."

"Have fun." Mrs. Matson closed the screen door and went back into the house. "Checkbook," she mumbled.

"That reminds me," Tracy said. "How are we going to earn money for the fair?"

"Let's get the book out of your house," Casey suggested.

"The book?"

"The book you took out of the library, *ma chère. Earning Money.*"

"Are you crazy, Casey Valentine? I didn't take a book out about money. I took one out about a girl— I forget her name. And the other one was—" She closed her mouth over her own words. *Earning Money. Early Monkeys.* She had read the title wrong!

Suppose she had mentioned monkeys to Casey! If she had, Casey would realize she couldn't read well. And that was one thing Casey wouldn't ever have to know. By the time Tracy was back in school and the Chickadees reading group, Casey would be in the city again.

"The book was *Earning Money,*" Casey repeated.

"I completely forgot," Tracy said. "You're right."

"Let's go get it then. Come on." Casey jumped to her feet.

"Sit down a minute." Tracy fanned herself vigorously. "It's too hot to be jumping around like a Mexican jumping bean."

Casey ran her tongue over her braces. "I thought you were in such a hurry to earn money."

"I am. It's just that I'm melting in this heat. Let's try to think of a way to earn money here, in the shade." She patted the step next to her. "If we can't think of anything, then we'll go upstairs to get the book."

"All right," Casey agreed.

They sat there looking into space for the next few minutes. Tracy tried desperately to think of some-

thing. Casey wouldn't be satisfied sitting there much longer. And if Casey made her bring down the book, she'd find out in about three and a half minutes just what kind of a reader Tracy was.

"We could get some paint and brushes," Casey said, "and make pictures of the scenery. You know, the mountains or the river."

"Don't need pictures of that," Tracy said. "They can look out the window—"

"Or how about baking some cookies and selling them?" Casey broke in.

"I tried that last year. But they turned out black on the bottom. I stuck icing all over them so you couldn't tell. But when Poopsie and Paul Stewart tasted them, they made me give the money back."

Casey laughed. "And I guess Poopsie would tell Leroy not to buy from us this year then. Anyway it's too hot to cook. How about baby-sitting?"

Tracy squinted her eyes, considering the idea. "Not bad."

"Do you think people will think we're too young?"

"Maybe we could do it during the daytime," Tracy answered. "But there's another problem. The only kid young enough to need a baby-sitter in High Flats is Bobby Schaefer."

"What's wrong with Bobby Schaefer?" Casey asked. "I wouldn't mind taking care of him."

Tracy giggled. "There's nothing wrong with Bobby. At least his mother doesn't think so. But Mrs. Schaefer thinks there's something wrong with me."

Casey looked mystified. "What do you mean?"

"Well—" Tracy paused to pluck a mint leaf from the plant growing next to the steps—"before summer va-

cation Mrs. Schaefer asked me to watch Bobby after school every day so she could get some housework done. She was going to give me a quarter a day."

"Sounds good to me," Casey said.

"Sounded good to me too. But it wasn't an easy job." Tracy frowned, remembering how hard it was chasing Bobby Schaefer up and down High Flats Road. "No, sir," she repeated, "not an easy job at all."

"But this time there would be two of us to do the work," Casey reminded her.

"If Mrs. Schaefer has forgotten—"

"What?"

"The first day nothing happened except that Bobby ran my legs off. But the second day was cool. The wind was blowing across the river. It was the kind of day you knew the trout would bite. I was dying to go fishing. Just dying."

"So?"

"So I decided to take that little monster up on the bridge with me. I took a ton of candy so he'd stay there. In no time he was slathered with chocolate. It was on his shirt and his arms and legs and all over his face. Then he got tired of the candy and ate the bait."

"The bait?" Casey repeated.

"Two worms and a fat green frog."

"What did you do?"

"I was afraid he'd get sick or something, so I told Mrs. Schaefer. She practically fainted. The whole time Bobby was screaming that he wanted more. And," she confessed, "I couldn't stop laughing."

"No wonder she thought something was wrong with you," Casey said, giggling.

"Yup. The doctor said it was all right, though. Said

lots of people in the world eat worms and frogs. Not a thing wrong with them."

"Wow." Casey shuddered.

"But maybe Mrs. Schaefer forgot about it. Let's go see."

A few minutes later they rang Mrs. Schaefer's bell.

"Up here," she called. She was shaking a mop out of an upstairs window.

"We were wondering," Tracy said, "do you need anyone to watch Bobby for you?"

"You?"

"There are two of us this time."

"That's twice as much bait for Bobby to eat," said Mrs. Schaefer. "Thank you, but no. I'm sorry, girls."

Bobby poked his head out of the window next to Mrs. Schaefer.

"I waked up," he said. "Mama and Bobby going to play now."

"Oh, Bobby," his mother said, "I have work to do." She gave her mop a final shake.

"Then Bobby play with girls," he said.

"I've just changed my mind," Mrs. Schaefer said. "I'll pay you each twenty-five cents every afternoon that you watch Bobby for an hour. But remember—"

"I know"—Tracy interrupted—"no frogs." She tried to figure how much money she could earn this way before school started. Not enough for the fair, and not enough to give the new principal, but it was a start. Definitely a start.

"No worms either," said Mrs. Schaefer.

"Don't worry," Casey said. "We'll be careful."

"I hope so," said Mrs. Schaefer. "Run downstairs to the girls, Bobby. Be a good boy."

Bobby's head disappeared from the window. In no time at all he was banging out the front door. He clattered down the front steps, dragging a box behind him.

"What have you got there?" Tracy asked.

Bobby lifted his blond curly head and pursed his lips together. "Things," he said.

Tracy looked at the box doubtfully. "Mrs. Schaefer, do you know that Bobby has a box full of nail polish bottles and lipstick?" she called.

Mrs. Schaefer poked her head out of the window again. "Take that away from him, Tracy," she said. "Bobby, you know you're not supposed to play with that stuff."

"That's Bobby for you," Tracy muttered to Casey under her breath.

Bobby wrapped his plump arms around the box. "Bobby needs this."

"You're going to get that nail polish all over the place." Tracy grabbed one end of the box. "Give it to me."

"Wait a minute, Tracy," Casey said.

Bobby let go of his end of the box. Tracy tried to keep her balance, but her foot slipped on one of Bobby's marbles. She tumbled backward into a sticker bush. The box flew through the air, spilling bottles over the grass.

"Ouch," Tracy said, dragging herself out of the bush. She held her breath. "Did anything break?"

"No. We were lucky." Casey bent down to pick up the bottles. "Help me, please," she asked Bobby.

Bobby let go of his end of the box.

Obediently he knelt in the grass and dumped bottles into the box.

Tracy whistled in surprise. "He listens to somebody!"

"I tried to tell you that you were just getting him madder, hurting his feelings."

Tracy felt her face redden. "Sorry," she mumbled. She picked up the box and put it next to the front door.

"Come on," she said to Bobby and held out her hand.

Bobby put his hands behind his back. "Not Tracy's hand." He held out his hand to Casey, and she took it.

"I think I have an old coloring book and some crayons at home," Tracy said.

"Good idea," said Casey. "Bobby can play with that and we can play the word game."

Bobby watched Tracy for a minute. "Coloring book," he said, and held out his other hand to Tracy.

Five minutes later they were settled on the grass at the bottom of Tracy's back steps. Bobby was making sweeping purple lines across the cover of the coloring book.

"Inside," Tracy said. "Color the inside pages."

"No," he said.

"Suit yourself."

Just then Leroy popped his head around the corner of the house. "Hey, Tracy," he called. "Can I borrow your wagon?"

Tracy felt her heart flop over. That was one wagon she could do without seeing again. "What do you want that old thing for?" she asked.

"I have a job. I'm earning money for the fair."

"What are you doing?"

"Mr. Lawrence at the quarry is letting me pile up the pieces of slate that are too small for him to bother with. Now Mr. Jensen is building a path in back of his house. He said he'd buy those little pieces from me, but I need your wagon to pull them down from the quarry."

"Not today," Tracy answered.

"Tracy!" Casey said in surprise. "He needs some money for the fair too."

Tracy looked at Casey. "I don't know where it is. I'll look around for it."

"When?" Leroy asked.

She waved her hand. "Soon," she replied vaguely.

"Come on, Tracy," he said. "I really need it."

As she tried to think of an excuse, Poopsie Pomeranz danced around the side of the house to the back. "I know where your wagon is," she said.

Trust Poopsie to be around at the wrong time, Tracy thought.

"Don't you remember the day you painted it?" Poopsie continued.

"I guess so." Tracy stood up. "I think it's in the garage. I'll get it."

12

It wasn't till Monday that Tracy got around to trying to read *Earning Money*. She knew nine words on the first page and twelve on the second. "I need more money," she said to Rebel, who was curled up beside her on the living room floor. "Baby-sitting for Bobby just isn't enough."

She spilled a bunch of vanilla cookies out of a cardboard box and lined them up in a row on the carpet. "Don't eat too fast," she warned the dog. "We're supposed to share." Usually Rebel was like a vacuum cleaner when it came to cookies. He'd sort of snuffle, and a whole pile would disappear.

But today he sniffed at the cookies and went back to sleep.

Tracy turned to the book. "Impossible," she muttered. She stood up, stretched, and walked over to look out the front door. Poopsie Pomerantz was running up

High Flats Road on tiptoe, her hands stretched high over her head. A handkerchief was tied over her nose and mouth.

Tracy banged the screen door open. "Could I ask what you're doing, Poopsie?" she called.

Poopsie stopped running and pulled off the handkerchief. "You mean this?" she asked, waving it in front of her. "I'm not supposed to get any dust in my nose. When I go fast—"

"No," Tracy interrupted. "I mean why are you running so peculiarly."

"Running?" Poopsie looked hurt. "I'm doing ballet. Look." She twirled around a couple of times, her arm curved upward with one finger dangling over her head. "Makes me a little dizzy," she panted.

"Some ballet," Tracy commented.

"Good, huh? I've really been practicing."

Tracy closed the screen door. "Thinks she's some kind of an actress," she said to Rebel.

Halfway across the living room floor she stopped and stood still. "That's it," she shouted. "We'll do a play."

She stooped down to pick the book up and tossed it under the couch. "Solves all our problems. Casey will forget about this stupid book and we'll probably make a fortune."

She dumped another pile of cookies on the floor for the dog and emptied the rest of the box into her pockets. "See you later, Rebel," she said over her shoulder and dashed out the front door.

By this time Poopsie had reached her house and seemed to be hopping back and forth on her front path.

"Hang around, Poopsie," Tracy shouted. "I may need you in a little while."

"Sure, Tracy, sure. I'm not doing anything. Where are you going?" Poopsie started down the path toward her.

"I don't need you yet. I mean later."

"Are you sure?"

"Very." She turned her back on Poopsie and raced down to Mrs. Clausson's to call for Casey.

"Come on out," she shouted. "Hurry up."

Casey poked her head out the door. "It's not time to get Bobby yet, is it?"

"No, we have a few minutes. But listen. I know a terrific way to make money."

"Did you read it in the book?" Casey asked, coming out on the porch.

"No. Thought it up all by myself. We'll put on a play. Get all the kids in it . . . me and you and Leroy and Richard and Poopsie. We'll practice for a couple of days and then we'll invite the whole round world to see it."

"What are we going to do with Bobby while we practice?"

"Stick him right in the middle of the whole thing. Give him a part. Means his mother and father will come to see it. More money for us."

Casey nodded. "Do you think Leroy and Richard will want to be in it?"

"Probably not." Tracy frowned. "They always have to gum up the works somehow. But let's go ask."

Together they walked up High Flats Road. Leroy was crossing the bridge, pulling Tracy's wagon filled with slate.

"This is your lucky day, Leroy!" Tracy stood in the

middle of the bridge so he'd have to stop and listen to her.

"Now what?" Leroy dropped the handle of the wagon and wiped his hands on his dungarees.

"You probably won't have enough money to spend at the fair just by selling that slate. Right?"

Leroy didn't answer, but from the look on his face, Tracy knew she was right.

"Thought so. Well, I have a way to solve all your problems. We're going to put on a play." Tracy narrowed her eyes. "Now I guess you don't have too much acting ability, Leroy. But I don't like to leave you out."

Leroy picked up the handle of the wagon. "Boy, are you good to me, Tracy!" He started to walk to the end of the bridge.

"Not so fast. Have you picked up all the slate or do you have some more trips to make?"

Leroy stopped again. "Three or four more trips should do it, I guess."

Tracy clicked her teeth. "Too bad. I need my wagon."

"What?"

"That's right, Leroy. I need my wagon. Now."

"You haven't used that wagon in months. You're just saying that so I'll be in your stupid play."

She smiled. "I guess you might say that."

"Sometimes I can't stand you, Tracy." Leroy glared at her.

"Will you be in the play?"

"Can I keep the wagon for a couple of days?"

She nodded. "Hurry up and get rid of that slate. We'll meet you in my backyard."

She turned to Casey. "Why don't you get Bobby while I get things set up at my house?"

She skipped off the bridge and started down High Flats Road. When she saw Poopsie sitting on her lawn, she stuck her fingers in her mouth and whistled piercingly.

Poopsie covered her ears and looked up. "Now, Tracy?"

"Now. Come on over."

Ten minutes later Tracy stood on the top of her back steps. "Listen, you guys," she said to Leroy and Richard, who were wrestling on the ground. "We've got to get serious. First of all, we'll have to take turns watching Bobby, or the next thing you know he'll be sitting in the middle of the river."

Leroy untangled himself from Richard. "How come we have to watch him? You and Casey are getting paid for baby-sitting."

"Look, Leroy," Tracy answered in a reasonable voice, "we can't be expected to do everything—run the whole play and baby-sit too."

"Let someone else run the play then," Leroy said.

"It was our idea," Casey said.

"Let's not waste another minute fighting," Tracy said. "By the time we get this play going, the fair will be over."

"What kind of a play is this going to be anyway?" Poopsie asked.

"Maybe I could write one," Casey said. "A mystery or something."

"We really don't have time for that," Tracy said. Then, seeing how disappointed Casey looked, she added, "Even though it probably would have been

great." She turned back to Poopsie. "We'll do an adventure. Let's play that I'm the star and . . ."

"I figured that," Leroy muttered to Richard under his breath.

"Some star," Richard snickered. "She'd better wear a mask."

"Come on, Richard," Tracy said. "I don't want to have to kick you out of here."

"I'm not even in the play," he answered. "I'm just watching."

"Too bad. I was going to give you a good part. Besides, think of all the money for the fair."

Richard thought for a minute. "Well, I guess so."

"It's settled then," Tracy said. "Leroy, you stand over on the side with your arms out. And hold still."

"What for?"

"You can be a tree. I come riding through the forest and . . ."

"A tree?" Leroy stuck his lower lip out. "A tree!" he repeated. "You must think I'm crazy. Do you think my mother and father will spend their good money to come and watch me be a tree?"

Tracy ignored him. "And then my horse stumbles over a rock. That's you, Poopsie. Curl yourself up near Leroy."

Poopsie looked up. "I was hoping to get to do a little ballet, Tracy. After all my lessons I should be dancing."

Tracy looked at her thoughtfully. "All right. You can be a butterfly. Dance around Leroy for a while."

"Me next, Tracy," Bobby said. "Me next."

"You can be the rock. Sit next to Leroy."

"Wait a minute, Tracy." Leroy jumped up and down in anger. "If you think I'm going to be a tree and the

rest of us a bunch of rocks and butterflies so you can be the whole play, you're out of your mind. Next you'll be telling Casey she can be the grass."

Richard rolled his eyes. "That's better than being Tracy's horse. How would you like that job?"

"I think Leroy's right," Casey said quietly. "I'd like to have a talking part."

"I'm doing the best I can," Tracy said in a hurt voice. "It's not easy thinking up this whole thing."

"You don't have to think of the whole thing, Tracy," Casey said. "I have a book of plays at Mrs. Clausson's house. We could pick one out and copy our parts. We'd have a real play then."

"Best idea I've heard all day," Richard said. "Go get the book."

"Right. Now we're getting somewhere," Leroy said, smirking at Tracy as Casey disappeared around the side of the house. "Guess who's going to have a little trouble reading her part, Richard?"

Richard started to flap his arms. "Peep, peep. I know who," he answered. "The chickadee herself. Old Tracy Matson."

13

Tracy sank down on the top step and picked at the peeling railing with her fingernail. By the time Casey rounded the corner of the house with the book of plays under her arm, Tracy had peeled a capital T in the post and had started on an M.

Casey settled herself on the lawn. "Let's see," she said, "we need a play with about six parts. Come on, Tracy." She patted the grass next to her. "Sit here and help me find one."

"In a minute." Tracy lowered her head and worked on the M. Her heart was beating so fast she could hardly catch her breath.

"Never mind," Poopsie said. "I'll help you." She leaned over Casey's shoulder. "Try to find something with dancing in it. That's kind of my specialty."

"We can add a dancing part for you," Casey said. "How about Cinderella?"

Tracy looked up. "Great idea," she said. She really wouldn't have to read that part out of the book. "Yes," she nodded. "I'll be Cind—"

"That's out," Leroy interrupted. "If you think I'm going to be a dwarf—"

"Typical of you, Leroy," said Tracy. "Can't even keep your fairy tales straight. Cinderella doesn't have dwarfs. She has a pumpkin and a fairy godmother."

"Well, don't think I'm going to be a pumpkin either."

"Would you rather be a fairy godmother?" Richard said. He rolled on the grass, laughing.

Leroy glared at him and then at Tracy, who was snickering. "At least I can read the parts," he said.

Casey looked at them curiously. "What's that supposed to mean?" she asked.

"Nothing," Tracy said. "Don't pay any attention to that idiot."

"If you two keep fighting, we'll never get this play going," Casey said. "Let me look for something else."

"With dancing," reminded Poopsie.

"With a little action," Leroy said.

"Here's a good one, I think . . . a mystery. Last year the fifth grade in my school did it."

"With spies?" Leroy asked.

"No, it's a detective kind. Are you coming over here, Tracy?"

Reluctantly Tracy got to her feet. "A detective mystery seems pretty silly to me," she said, walking over to Casey.

"Why?"

"I really don't see Leroy or Richard as the lead in the play. I should be the star. Besides, made-up plays are more fun to do."

"You sound as if you knew everything," Leroy said, "but I know why you don't want to do that play. You . . ."

Casey swished her breath through her braces. "Just try. Come on. We'll read the parts together, and if you don't like it, we'll try something else."

"I'm getting sick of this whole play idea," Tracy said. "How about a little swim instead? Or we could go fishing. Catch us a couple of pickerel."

"No." Leroy smirked at her. "Let's read the play."

"It's too hot," she said. "I'm going to die of this heat if we don't cool off first." She fanned her hand in front of her face.

Casey thrust the book in her hand. "It'll take only five minutes. Then we'll go for a swim. Just think of the fair and all that money."

Tracy stared at the book in her hand.

"What's the matter, Tracy?" Leroy asked. "Too hard for you to read?"

Casey looked at Tracy.

Richard laughed. "You might say Tracy can't read anything."

"She can so," Leroy said. "She can read *Go and Run*."

"Go, go, go," Richard said in a high babyish voice. "Run, run, run."

"I can read better than that—" Tracy began and broke off.

"I thought you loved to read," Casey said. "Why didn't you tell me? I would have helped you with it the way you helped me with the rowing."

Tracy lowered her head. She wished she could disappear. "I don't want any help," she said.

"You need more than help," Richard said, laughing. "You need a new brain."

Tracy stood up. She was afraid she was going to cry. "Go away," she said. "Get out of my yard. All of you."

Casey looked at her. For a minute she looked as if she were going to say something.

"Get out of here!" Tracy yelled.

Casey took Bobby by the hand and followed Poopsie and the boys out of the yard.

"You forgot your book," Tracy called. She tried to sound as if nothing had happened. "You better take it with you."

Casey didn't answer. She didn't even turn around. She walked down the street, leaving Tracy standing there watching, the book in her hand.

Tracy went slowly up the back steps into the house. "Think I'll find Rebel," she said to herself. "I've been neglecting that poor dog lately. I'd better make it up to him. Only friend I have."

Looking out the window, she watched Casey and the others disappear down High Flats Road. What a terrible thing, she thought, never to have any friends. All the things she'd planned weren't going to happen. Leroy would never be her friend. And Casey probably wouldn't ever come back to High Flats.

And it was all because of the reading.

She walked slowly into the living room. "Lazy dog," she said.

Rebel was in the same spot he had been when Tracy left this morning. "You didn't even eat your cookies."

She lay down and buried her head in Rebel's fur. "Just let me lie here for a minute, then I'll feel better."

Rebel curled his broad pink tongue out over Tracy's hand and rested his chin on her wrist.

Tracy sat up in surprise. "Boy, is your nose dry," she said. "Hot, too." She looked at him carefully. Rebel's coat looked different. Usually his wiry black hair gleamed, but now it was dusty, dirty almost, and gray.

She turned the dog's head toward her. Rebel's eyes looked dull too. "Wait a minute," she said and ran to the telephone. Her mother's number at work was taped to the bottom.

She dialed, still watching Rebel.

"Mr. Parrish," she said to the man who answered the phone, "this is Tracy Matson. Would you get my mother, please?"

"She's not here, Tracy. I'm sorry," Mr. Parrish said. "Someone said she went out for lunch today."

"But I need her now," Tracy insisted. "Where did she go?"

"I really don't know," he said. "But she'll be back by one o'clock. Call her then."

Tracy heard the receiver click. Then she went to the front door to look for Leroy. Maybe he'd know what to do about Rebel.

Leroy wasn't in front of his house, but Mrs. Bemus was pulling into her driveway. Tracy ran out and down High Flats Road. By this time Mrs. Bemus was struggling into her house with a package of groceries.

"Please," Tracy called. "I think my dog is sick." She stopped. She didn't even know what she wanted Mrs. Bemus to do. But Mrs. Bemus seemed to know. She put the groceries on the front step, not even stopping to pick up the two oranges that rolled down the step and onto the grass.

"Do you think he's going to die?" Tracy asked.

"Let's have a look," she said and followed Tracy back to her house. In the living room she knelt down next to Rebel and gently rubbed his ear.

"Tracy," she said, "I think he's pretty sick. I bet you know where a good veterinarian is around here."

"Dr. Wayne. He's just over the mountain . . . in Windsor."

Mrs. Bemus nodded. "I'll get my car. Can you carry him outside alone? Or do you want me to help?"

"I can get him." Tracy looked at her gratefully.

"I'll be right back," Mrs. Bemus said. "I'll pull the car up your driveway."

Tracy lifted Rebel off the living room floor. "Come on, old boy," she said. "We'll get Dr. Wayne to make you better."

But in the car she wasn't so sure. Rebel lay across her lap and never moved during the trip.

"Do you think he's going to die?" she asked Mrs. Bemus. The words caught in her throat so that they came out strangely. "If he does die, it's probably my fault. I haven't done one thing right this summer."

"We're not going to worry about that now," Mrs. Bemus said, flashing a smile at her. "We're going to worry about getting across this mountain in my crazy old car."

14

The trip seemed to take forever. Mrs. Bemus slowed down to a crawl every time she came to a curve in the mountain. She'd have to get used to country roads, Tracy thought.

Finally Mrs. Bemus stopped in front of Dr. Wayne's office. "Hop out with What's-his-name," she said. "I'll park in the back."

"Rebel," Tracy said. She slipped out of the car and carried the dog into the doctor's office.

Mrs. Wayne was in the reception room, watering some plants in the window. Tracy wondered why she bothered. The plants looked like a bunch of dead strings.

"What's the matter, Tracy?" she asked. "Rebel sick?" She clicked her teeth sympathetically. "Take him right back in. The doctor's in his office."

Dr. Wayne looked over his glasses at Tracy as she

laid Rebel on the table. "I see you never put him on a diet." He shook his head.

Tracy leaned against the metal table. It was cold against her midriff. The blinds were drawn in the office. The room seemed dark and gloomy. She shivered.

Rebel was shivering too. He rolled his eyes back at her. As usual, he was terrified of the veterinarian.

"Don't be afraid," Tracy crooned to him. She looked anxiously at the doctor. But Dr. Wayne wasn't paying attention to her. He was touching Rebel carefully, looking in his eyes and ears and listening to his heart with the stethoscope.

Finally he looked up. "What have you fed the dog lately?"

"Let's see." Tracy tried to remember. "We had cookies this morning, but I don't think Rebel ate any. We had a two-stick orange ice after breakfast, one stick each. For supper last night my mother gave him dog food."

For a minute she was tempted not to tell what she and Rebel had eaten for a snack last night, but then she sighed and rushed through the rest of the list. "Two pretzels, one each, a peanut butter sandwich, and four gum drops." Remembering, Tracy had to smile a little. She loved to watch Rebel eat gum drops. He had such a job yanking his teeth apart when they were glued together with sticky candy. "Oh, and I almost forgot. Half a—"

"Enough," Dr. Wayne interrupted. "An upset stomach. It's a wonder you don't have one too. When are you going to listen to me? That dog needs a healthy diet. Do you think you know more than I do?"

She shook her head and looked down at the black-and-white squares on the floor.

"I'm going to give you some medicine to soothe his stomach. Give it to him three times today and tomorrow. And *never* feed him sugar or junk food."

Tracy eased her hands under Rebel's quivering body and managed to take the medicine from Dr. Wayne. Still looking at the linoleum floor, she backed out of the room.

Mrs. Bemus was waiting in the reception room. "Is he all right?" she asked.

"He has an upset stomach."

Mrs. Bemus put her hand on Tracy's shoulder. "Do you need money to pay the doctor?"

"No. He'll send the bill to my mother."

On the way home Tracy leaned her head back against the seat. It had been a long morning.

"I bet you can't wait to get home," Mrs. Bemus said. "What are the other kids doing on such a beautiful day?"

Tracy had almost forgotten. Casey and everybody else were probably at Leroy's doing the play. Without her.

"I think they're putting on a play. Everyone is trying to get money for the fair," she said. She tried to think of something to say that would change the subject. Finally she cleared her throat. "Thank you for taking me to Dr. Wayne. I was really worried about Rebel."

"Glad to do it, Tracy. You've been such a help to me."

She glanced at Mrs. Bemus to see if she was serious. "I've been a help?" Some help, she thought to herself.

"I found fish for my cat on the back porch three times this week," Mrs. Bemus replied.

"I owed you," Tracy said without thinking.

Mrs. Bemus glanced at her. "How could you owe me?"

For several seconds there was silence. Tracy couldn't think of one thing to say.

"Tracy?" Mrs. Bemus asked.

Tracy searched around in her mind for an answer. For some reason, she pictured Casey in front of her house yelling up at her, "The worst rower in the world is here." If only she had yelled down, "The worst reader in the world is here."

By now Mrs. Bemus was driving up High Flats Road. As they pulled to a stop in front of her house, Tracy reached for the handle. Before she could stop herself, the words burst out. "I'm the lunatic who painted your house." She opened the car door. "And my reading's a mess too."

Mrs. Bemus looked at her gravely. "Why don't you put Rebel inside? Then come down to my house. We'll talk about it."

Tracy lifted Rebel out of the car and closed the door with her hip. She looked at Mrs. Bemus and nodded, then turned and trudged up her front path.

Inside, she laid Rebel gently on the living room rug. "You'll be all right," she said. "Don't worry, old boy." She straightened up. "I have to see Mrs. Bemus, but I'll be back soon." She gulped. "I hope."

Her hands felt sweaty. She wiped them on the back of her shorts. She wondered if Mrs. Bemus would expel her, and what her mother and father would say.

She opened the door and walked down High Flats

Road, head hanging. She'd die if she met one of the kids now. But there was no one around except the two old men rocking on Mrs. Clausson's porch.

Mrs. Bemus was waiting for her. Before Tracy could even ring the bell, the screen door swung open. "Come on in the kitchen," Mrs. Bemus said.

Tracy blinked. The house was dark and cool after the sun on High Flats Road. She edged herself into a chair at the kitchen table.

Mrs. Bemus slid a plate of cookies over to her. "Now," she said, "let's talk."

Tracy looked at the cookies for a moment. Chocolate fudge. But her mouth was so dry she wouldn't be able to swallow one if she chewed for a hundred years.

"I didn't mean . . ." Tracy began. "I couldn't read the label. . . . I mean, I just wanted to fix the house up. Smooth it out with turpentine. But the paint can said Turkey Red." She glanced at Mrs. Bemus. But all she could see was the top of her head. Mrs. Bemus seemed to be staring at the floor.

Tracy began again. "All because I can't read. It's such a waste of time. If I didn't have to read, everything would be perfect." She swallowed hard. "Casey isn't going to be my friend anymore and Leroy thinks I'm dumb. I'm not even going to be in the play, and it was all my idea. . . ." Her voice trailed off.

"All this happened because you're having trouble with reading?" Mrs. Bemus asked.

Tracy nodded solemnly. "Makes me get into all kinds of messes."

"That's why you and Casey aren't friends anymore?"

"Well," she said reluctantly, "Casey did say she'd help me with the reading."

"If I didn't have to read, everything would be perfect."

"When is she going to start?"

Tracy lowered her head. "I told her I didn't want her help."

"Oh." Mrs. Bemus looked at her thoughtfully. "And Leroy?"

"He keeps peeping and flapping his arms around just because I'm in the Chickadees reading group. Thinks he's so smart."

"Isn't he the boy you told me about? The one who doesn't know anything? The idiot?"

Tracy felt her face redden. It sounded as if she were as mean as old Leroy. Meaner.

"All this because you're having trouble with reading," Mrs. Bemus said again.

"I . . ." Tracy said and hesitated. Somehow that seemed a little backward. She was blaming all her problems on reading. The truth was she was too lazy to sit around practicing her reading and tried to make up for it by acting as if she knew everything in the whole round world. She took a deep breath. "I'm really sorry about your house. I was going to earn about a hundred dollars with the play. Give you a whole bunch of money to get the house painted again."

Mrs. Bemus reached over and took a cookie. "A little stale," she said, "but not bad. You know, Tracy, I'm getting used to the house. No one else around here has red cabbages painted on the shutters."

"Cabbages!" Tracy exclaimed. "Is that what you think? They were supposed to be roses."

Mrs. Bemus stared off into space. "Yes. I can see that now. I think I'll keep them. I'll give the front door a couple of dabs of paint and leave the shutters alone."

Tracy stood up. "I guess I could practice being a better artist."

Mrs. Bemus sat there for a few minutes. Then her eyes began to twinkle. "What about being a garage painter? I didn't have the garage painted with the house. Since it's in the back, not too many people see it. It wouldn't make much difference if you made a couple of mistakes. If you and some of those friends of yours want to make some money for the fair, I'd like to have you do it for me."

"Do you mean it? You could just pay the rest of the kids. I won't take a salary. Kind of make up for the first mess."

"That seems fair," Mrs. Bemus said. "Round up the kids after lunch and let me know when you're ready to begin."

15

Back in her own kitchen, Tracy put Rebel on his rug under the table and sank down on a chair. "Round up the kids," she said with a moan. "Now how am I going to do that when not one kid in High Flats wants to talk to me? Just about get one problem solved and another one pops up."

She wet the tip of her finger with her tongue and picked up a few Crispies that were left on the table from breakfast. She could picture all the kids racing off to the fair, pockets bulging with money, while she was home sitting in a chair reading a baby book like *Go and Run*. The baby-sitting money from Bobby wouldn't even be enough to buy a decent snack. "My own fault," she said and shook herself. "Better fix some lunch and try to forget about the whole thing for a while."

She stood up. "Too bad, Rebel," she said firmly to the sleeping dog. "You're going to have thickish pink yuck for your snack. Just what the doctor ordered."

She rattled around in the drawers. "Not a decent thing in the house to eat unless you count a salt and pepper sandwich. Maybe the refrigerator . . ."

Behind her there was a sharp sound. Tracy jumped. "What was that?"

"Only me, blowing my nose," said Poopsie, leaning against the screen. "What did you think? A burglar or something?"

"What are you doing here, Poopsie? Why aren't you working on the play?"

Poopsie shrugged. "No play."

"How come?"

"Everybody's fighting and carrying on. Leroy wanted to do a play about cowboys and Richard wanted to be a spy. The whole time Casey kept yelling that everybody should wait awhile until she wrote a play. Finally everyone went home mad." Poopsie twirled around once. "Nobody gets things going around here without you. Even Leroy said so."

"Leroy?"

"Yeah. He said how come we can't even put on a stupid play without that crazy Tracy! And I said Tracy's not crazy. And he said he didn't mean it that way. So come on out now."

Funny, she hadn't cried once during this entire horrible day. But now that Poopsie had said something nice, she could feel the tears starting in her eyes. Turning so Poopsie couldn't see her face, she said gruffly, "I have to have my lunch now and feed Rebel. I'll see you in a little while."

Poopsie stood there for a minute, then skipped down
the back steps and out of the yard. As she turned the
corner of the house, Tracy yelled after her, "Hey
Poopsie. I meant to tell you . . ."

Poopsie hopped back a step and looked at Tracy
over her shoulder.

"Your ballet isn't bad at all for a six-year-old."

Poopsie beamed. "I just keep trying." She twirled
around and ran on tiptoe out of the yard. "I just keep
practicing, Tracy," she called as she rounded the
corner.

Tracy went back to the refrigerator and pulled out
a jar of marmalade. She reached into the drawer for a
spoon and quickly dipped it into the jar. "If I stop to
think about it or waste the rest of the afternoon on
lunch, I'll never get this over with," she told Rebel.
After two quick mouthfuls, she gave Rebel his medicine and was out the back door.

"I've got to start over. Make up with the kids. Get
my friends back. Can't act as if I know everything in
the whole round world." She chuckled to herself. "Just
about half."

First she took the garbage can and walked out behind the vegetable garden. For days now she had been
collecting overripe cucumbers. What a trick that would
have been, she thought. She would have dumped them
in the tall grass near Leroy's yard and waited for him
to come running out of it, convinced that a rattler was
hanging around just waiting to get him.

She dumped the cucumbers into the can with a
spade, still thinking about Leroy's face if he had ever
smelled those cucumbers. No more tricks, she said to
herself. At least, she amended, not the hurting kind.

She straightened up and crossed the street to Leroy's. She stood there for a moment, embarrassed. Finally she called out, "Hey, Leroy?"

No one answered.

She walked through the tall grass around the side of the house. "Leroy," she called again. "Are you back there?"

Leroy and Richard came around the side of the house. "The chickadee herself," Richard said.

Tracy ran her tongue over her lips. "I know I'm a pretty bad reader, Richard, but I just wish you'd stop reminding me."

Richard stood there, mouth open. "I thought you were the expert of High Flats," he said after a moment.

"Shut up a minute, Rich," Leroy said. "What do you want Tracy?"

"I heard the play is off."

Leroy nodded.

"Want to paint Mrs. Bemus's garage with me? For money?"

Leroy stood there, considering. "I suppose you'll be the boss."

"Well, I got the job," she began, and then paused. "But, I don't have to be the boss."

"All right," Leroy said. "Sure."

"How about getting Poopsie?" Tracy said. "We need all the hands we can get. Then go down to Mrs. Bemus's garage and wait for me. I have to go see Casey."

She started for Mrs. Clausson's and stopped. "Leroy," she said, "I just thought of something. How about we start over with the play when we finish the garage? Double the money that way."

They raced toward Mrs. Bemus's house.

"Why not?" Leroy said. "We may turn out to be rich yet."

"At least," she said, "rich enough to get me to the fair."

She turned up Mrs. Clausson's walk and stopped, suddenly afraid. Casey must think she was a terrible dummy. It was no good. She might as well turn right around. There wasn't a thing she could say. She stood there for a minute, thinking. Yes, she guessed there was, and she was going to say it right now.

"Casey," she shouted.

Casey popped her head out of an upstairs window.

"Casey," she said again. "I'm sorry about everything. I really do need some help, after all."

"Be right down."

Tracy grinned. "How would you like me to teach you how to paint a garage?"

Casey grinned back. "How would you like me to teach you how to read?"

Tracy thought for a minute. She remembered the book with the girl on the cover. And the piece of paper in her dresser drawer. The one with all the minutes she owed. It would certainly be a relief to work some of that off. "I'd like you to help me," she said. "I really would."

And while she was at it, Tracy thought, she'd get to her closet one of these days. Clean the whole mess up. A new beginning.

Then she shook herself. "Hurry up. Those boys will start to paint without us. And they don't know how to do it the right way. We have to get down there now."

Casey came down the steps. Tracy grabbed her hand and together they raced toward Mrs. Bemus's house.